Praise for *Diary of a Wimpy Vampire: Because the Undead* Have Feelings Too and *Diary of a Wimpy Vampire: Prince of Dorkness*

'Please ... this series of vampire parodies is one of the funniest I've ever read.'
wondrousreads.com

'Fantastically witty and hugely entertaining, this fun and accessible diary will appeal to any fan of *Twilight* or Adrian Mole, teenage or otherwise...'
Goodreads.com

'*Twilight* meets *Diary of a Wimpy Kid* in this inventive parody of both.'
guardianbookshop.co.uk

'This hilarious book will have you laughing your head off as you learn of the misfortune of Nigel Mullet.'
Fresh Direction

'Teens who are fans of the *Twilight* saga will love this laugh-out-loud parody.'
Woman's Way

'A funny light-hearted read which touches on first love.'
Books 4 Teens

Diary of a Wimpy Vampire won the Manchester Fiction City Award and the Lincolnshire Young People's Book Award, and was short-listed for the Northern Ireland Book Award, the Worcestershire Teen Book Award and the Hampshire Book Award.

The Wimpy Vampire strikes back

Tim Collins is originally from Manchester and now lives in London. He is the author of over twenty books including the *Wimpy Vampire* series. He has won the Manchester Fiction City award and the Lincolnshire Young People's Book Award, and his books have been translated into over thirty languages.

Find out more about Tim at his website:
www.timcollinsbooks.com

Also by Tim Collins

DIARY OF A WIMPY VAMPIRE: BECAUSE THE UNDEAD HAVE FEELINGS TOO

DIARY OF A WIMPY VAMPIRE: PRINCE OF DORKNESS

ADVENTURES OF A WIMPY WEREWOLF: HAIRY BUT NOT SCARY

THE DIARY OF DORKIUS MAXIMUS

DORKIUS MAXIMUS IN EGYPT

The Wimpy Vampire strikes back

Tim Collins

Michael O'Mara Books Limited

First published in Great Britain in 2013 by
Michael O'Mara Books Limited
9 Lion Yard
Tremadoc Road
London SW4 7NQ

Copyright © Michael O'Mara Books Limited 2013

All rights reserved. No part of this publication may be reproduced, stored
in a retrieval system, or transmitted by any means, without the prior
permission in writing of the publisher, nor be otherwise circulated in any
form of binding or cover other than that in which it is published and
without a similar condition including this condition being imposed on
the subsequent purchaser.

A CIP catalogue record for this book is available from
the British Library.

Papers used by Michael O'Mara Books Limited are natural,
recyclable products made from wood grown in sustainable forests.
The manufacturing processes conform to the environmental regulations
of the country of origin.

ISBN: 978-1-78243-022-3 in paperback print format
978-1-78243-041-4 in ePub format
978-1-78243-040-7 in Mobipocket format

1 3 5 7 9 10 8 6 4 2

www.mombooks.com
Designed and typeset by Envy Design

Illustrations by Andrew Pinder
Printed and bound by CPI Group (UK) Ltd, Croydon CR0 4YY

ACKNOWLEDGEMENTS

Thanks to Louise Dixon, Lindsay Davies,
Ana McLaughlin, Andrew Pinder, Collette Collins and
everyone at Michael O'Mara books.

WEDNESDAY 1ST JANUARY

Went to school, did my homework, drank some blood. Another typical day at our coven.

Mr Dashwood gave us a history lesson this morning. It was really boring, just an endless list of famous vampires, the dates they transformed and the ways they were destroyed.

I can still hear him droning on now. 'Staked, beheaded, fried. Staked, beheaded, survived...'

There was no reason for the lesson to be so dull. We've got such an amazing

array of vampires in our class we could learn more about history just by chatting.

Seth was transformed over 3,000 years ago in Egypt, Lenora was transformed over 150 years ago, and I've been a vampire since the early twentieth century. Imagine all the experiences we'd be able to share.

Instead, dull old Dashwood forces us to face the front and copy down his notes. If you so much as speak, he calls you up to the front and holy waters you. He's so old-fashioned.

THURSDAY 2ND JANUARY

The cleaner Mrs Dean came to dust my room this morning. She poured dust on my table, my coffin and my windowsill. It looks much better now.

I wish she'd do it more often, but I don't want to nag. Our

castle has eight floors and there are over sixty vampires living here in total, so she has a lot to do.

Our coven is situated on a secluded island off the coast of Scotland, so we have to go to the mainland to find humans to mesmerize and drain blood from. This evening Rob from the blood collection squad came back from his expedition with five barrels of type B+. Looks like he's been completely ignoring my ethical harvesting policy again.

When I took over as leader, I pledged to take no more than two pints from each human. This was to show that I'm a different type of coven boss, who looks on humans as friends rather than drink-vending machines.

Rob claims he's following my policy, but it tastes a lot like he's been draining entire barrels from single humans. The poor people he got it from must look like deflated balloons now.

Friday 3rd January

A couple of new vampires came to the coven today. Needless to say, it was my job to interview them. I picked up the Vampire Council guidebook and started going through all the questions:

'Are you carrying any wooden stakes, crucifixes or garlic bread?'

'Do you have reason to believe you're being hunted by a vampire slayer or paranormal romance fan?'

The Wimpy Vampire Strikes Back

'Is it possible a werewolf might have tampered with your bags?'

Of course everyone's going to answer 'no' to these questions. What's the point of asking them?

When I was appointed leader, I thought it would mean relaxing in my coffin while hot vampire girls like Lenora brought me crystal glasses filled to the brim with fresh blood. I didn't think it would mean writing endless reports and ploughing through silly guidebooks.

How can I be expected to cope with all this responsibility? I'm only fifteen. Well, technically I'm 102, but I was transformed at the age of fifteen, and I still look that age. I should be in my room playing computer games, not slogging through endless paperwork.

I got bored with the obvious questions and flipped to the back of the guidebook. It said I had to email info@vampirecouncil.com with the names of the newcomers and they'd let me know if they had criminal records. So what was I bothering with the interrogation for?

I told the new vampires they were welcome to join, pending feedback from the Vampire Council. I've put them in a room on the minus second floor for the time being.

One of the new vampires is a middle-aged woman called Svetlana who was wearing a red ball gown. The other is a young boy called Viktor who sat silently on her lap the whole

time. He was wearing a purple velvet suit with a matching cape and knee-length socks. He was pale even by vampire standards and had skin as white as a freshly brushed fang.

According to Svetlana, they're seeking asylum because they've been persecuted in human society. That's hardly surprising. At my old school in Stockfield, where I used to live amongst humans, you couldn't even get away with wearing trainers that were a couple of years old. You can't dress two centuries out of date and expect no one to say anything.

The Wimpy Vampire Strikes Back

9PM

I've just sent an email to the Vampire Council:

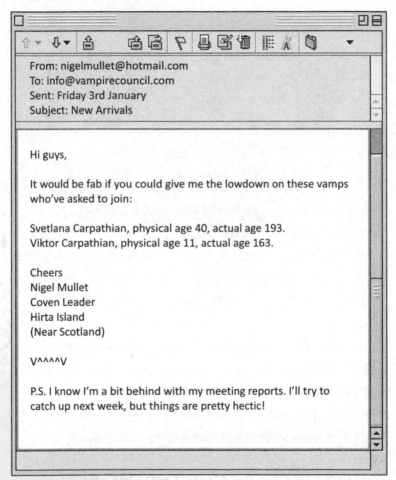

From: nigelmullet@hotmail.com
To: info@vampirecouncil.com
Sent: Friday 3rd January
Subject: New Arrivals

Hi guys,

It would be fab if you could give me the lowdown on these vamps who've asked to join:

Svetlana Carpathian, physical age 40, actual age 193.
Viktor Carpathian, physical age 11, actual age 163.

Cheers
Nigel Mullet
Coven Leader
Hirta Island
(Near Scotland)

V^^^^V

P.S. I know I'm a bit behind with my meeting reports. I'll try to catch up next week, but things are pretty hectic!

The Wimpy Vampire Strikes Back

SATURDAY 4TH JANUARY

School again today. On a *Saturday*. Unbelievable, eh? According to Mr Dashwood, we don't need days off because we don't sleep, so we get 'more than enough leisure time' at night. I don't. I've got all that leadership nonsense to cope with.

Mr Dashwood built the classroom in one of the ground-floor rooms when he joined the coven a century ago. I don't think he's been back to the human world since, which might explain why he thinks it's still acceptable to punish us all the time.

Today he called Seth up to the front for talking in class.

'I've warned you over and over again', said Mr Dashwood, straightening his mortarboard and flattening his gown. 'You've left me with no choice.'

Mr Dashwood took out his vial of holy water. Everyone lifted the fronts of their desks up to protect against splashes. He then unscrewed the top and flung the water onto Seth. I peered around my desk, waiting for Seth to scream and collapse to the floor. He just stood in silence as the water dripped down his bare chest onto his shendyt.

'You obviously want stronger punishment', said Mr Dashwood. He reached into the top drawer of his desk and took out a large black box.

There was a low hiss from the rest of the class. Seth was about to get crucifixed!

If a vampire so much as glimpses a religious symbol, they get a splitting headache. The punishment box is a barbaric invention that lets vampires show a crucifix to others without seeing it themselves. I'm surprised the Vampire Council allows it.

Mr Dashwood pointed the box at Seth and pulled down the screen on the front.

This time I was expecting Seth to collapse to the floor in agony. But he just shrugged. It was really weird.

'Imposter!' shouted

Mr Dashwood. He pointed to me. 'Summon the Circle of Elders! I have reason to believe this child isn't really a vampire at all!'

SUNDAY 5TH JANUARY

The Circle of Elders consists of my mum, my dad and an old man called Cecil who used to live with us.

I appointed them when I was put in charge, because I couldn't be bothered interviewing anyone else.

Tonight we took our chairs behind the large oak table in the discussion room on the top floor of the castle. Mr Dashwood and Seth stood in front of us.

'What charge do you bring before the elders?' asked Cecil. I'd already told him all about it. He was just milking it to sound important.

'This child cannot be a vampire,' said Mr Dashwood. 'I

doused him with holy water and crucifixed him and he didn't even flinch!

Dad took a blood flask out of his pocket, unscrewed it and carried it over to Seth. A pair of sharp fangs extended down from his teeth.

'He looks like one to me', said Dad.

'Appearances can be deceptive', said Cecil. He got up and paced back and forth with his hands behind his back. 'You're lucky I'm here today. I must be one of the few vampires still living who knows about these creatures.'

'What creatures?' asked Seth.

Cecil wandered over to him and prodded his forehead. 'What we have here is not a vampire, but a shapeshifter. He might look like a vampire today, but tomorrow he could resemble a snake, a sparrow or even a werewolf!'

Mum, Dad and Mr Dashwood jerked their heads back and hissed. I didn't join in because I'm not a complete and utter idiot.

'It's not true', shouted Seth, his eyes widening. 'I don't even know what a shapeshifter is.'

'Liar!' cried Mr Dashwood. 'Don't listen to the fraud!'

While all this was going on, I wandered out of the discussion room and down the stone stairwell to my sister's room, which is on the minus second floor.

She was out, so I barged in and tore down two of her posters, one featuring a fluffy kitten and another of Katy

Perry. I ripped out the cat's head and stuck it over the image of the pop starlet.

The Wimpy Vampire Strikes Back

By the time I got back inside the discussion room, Seth was sobbing and the others were discussing the safest way to destroy him.

I walked up to Seth and held out my picture of the cat's head on Katy Perry's body. He screamed and fell to his knees.

'What fresh devilry is this?' asked Mr Dashwood.

'Isn't it obvious?' I asked. 'Seth was transformed at a time when everyone worshipped gods with animal heads. So those are the things that distress him, not the symbols of newer religions such as Christianity.'

'Ah', said Mr Dashwood. 'That does make sense when you think about it.'

'It's just as I suspected', said Cecil.

That's right. It's just as he suspected except that it's the exact opposite of what he suspected.

Everyone just sloped off after that, leaving me to put the chairs away and make a start on the meeting report.

None of them thanked me for sorting it out. None of them apologized for being stupid. They just wandered down to the kitchen for their evening blood. Unbelievable.

MONDAY 6TH JANUARY

The thing that annoys me most about yesterday is how easy it was for Cecil to stir up hatred against Seth. We're always complaining that humans persecute us without attempting to understand us. Yet as soon as they thought Seth was a shapeshifter, Mum, Dad and Mr Dashwood were just as small-minded and vengeful as any torch-wielding villager. Much as I hate being in charge, I wouldn't trust any of that lot to take over.

11PM

I'm really tired and I can't even lie down on my bed because I haven't got one.

When we moved here from Stockfield, Dad refused to let me bring my bed, as he said all the rooms would already have them. And what did we find when we got here? Smelly coffins filled with soil. Apparently it's more 'traditional' and 'atmospheric.'

Why is everyone here so obsessed with tradition? It's not as though tourism's a big industry for our hidden, secret community.

Obviously, I don't sleep, so it's not a massive deal. But it would be nice to have somewhere to rest that made me feel like a valued, respected leader and not a smelly, malnourished zombie.

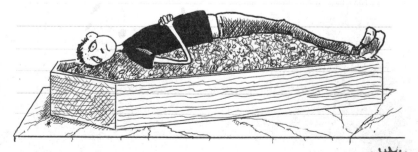

The Wimpy Vampire Strikes Back

TUESDAY 7TH JANUARY

This is ridiculous. When Mum called round today, I assumed she was going to apologize for her behaviour the other night, but all she did was tell me off for ripping up my sister's posters.

The Wimpy Vampire Strikes Back

As if those tacky posters matter. I had to act fast to save the life of an innocent vampire. I think that's worth more than a bit of tat from a gift shop.

I ended up having to go to my sister's room and apologize, which was ridiculous. I'm supposed to be the leader of one of the oldest vampire covens in Europe. I don't have time to grovel to brainless little brats.

Instead of simply accepting my apology, my sister called me a 'complete and utter human'. She should know better than to use that speciesist language, which she's obviously picked up from her friends Amber and Ellie.

Just a couple of years ago, we lived in a town full of humans and she was happy to mix with them. Now she hangs around with vampires, the word has suddenly become an insult. Her fickleness is astounding.

In the end I had to promise to get Rob, Mike and Henry to buy her a replacement Katy Perry poster next time they visit the mainland to get blood. I'm sure that's going to go down well. At least it will put vampire hunters off their scent. They'll never believe that any genuine supernatural creatures could be so lame.

1 OPM

I just called a meeting with Rob, Mike and Henry.

The three of them work on a rota to visit the mainland in small fishing boats and harvest blood from humans. Rob and

The Wimpy Vampire Strikes Back

Mike used to work as nightclub bouncers, and they both have shaved heads and wear leather jackets over shirts and ties. Henry used to work as a body snatcher and has thick sideburns and a black top hat.

Rob and Mike refused to buy the Katy Perry poster. They said it wouldn't be safe to visit human shops, but I think they were just ashamed. Henry was happy to do it, though. I gave him a tenner and showed him a picture of her on my laptop.

I warned him to be careful when browsing the racks. I once got a splitting headache looking at the poster for *Appetite for*

Destruction by Guns N' Roses because it had a massive cross in the middle. You'd think heavy metal bands of all people would be more courteous to us.

WEDNESDAY 8TH JANUARY

Cecil came into my room this afternoon to complain about Svetlana pushing to the front of the kitchen blood queue. He said that both those new vampires are very antisocial and should come out and talk to the rest of us.

Great to know this is somehow my problem. Who cares if they stay in their room all the time? They might just be shy.

10PM

I just made my way down to the new vampires' room to pass on Cecil's complaints.

'Come in', said Svetlana.

She was sitting in a rocking chair in the corner of the room, cradling Viktor in her arms. He was holding a blood-filled baby bottle with both hands, while she wiped stray flecks of blood from around his mouth.

'Who's a messy little boy?' crooned Svetlana.

It was pretty creepy. I know vampires are meant to be, but this was freaky even by our standards.

'Just checking how you're settling in', I said.

Viktor fixed his sunken eyes on me as he sucked from the bottle.

'What did the Vampire Council say?' asked Svetlana. 'You can't trust them, you know.'

I'd forgotten about that. I should probably get round to sending a follow-up email.

'I'm sure it's fine,' I said. 'But that's not what I wanted to talk about. Someone has claimed that you pushed to the front in the kitchen this morning, so I was wondering if you could stick to the queue from now on. We might be damned, but that doesn't mean we have to be damn rude, that's what we say here.'

I grinned awkwardly at Svetlana, but she just scowled at me. 'Viktor gets nervous if I leave him alone for too long. Especially if it's dark.'

'And don't be afraid to come out for a chat,' I said. 'We're quite a friendly bunch, you know. We don't bite!'

Svetlana and Viktor glared at me.

'Well, we do,' I said. 'But you get the idea!'

Not even a smile.

'But seriously,' I said. 'You're welcome to come to our school, Viktor. We start at nine every morning.'

'My son doesn't want to hear the lies of a buffoon with a blackboard,' said Svetlana. 'If he has any questions, he can ask me.'

I felt like I should defend Mr Dashwood, but she was sort of right.

'Or you could join the football team,' I said. 'We're playing on the field outside the main entrance tomorrow.'

The Wimpy Vampire Strikes Back

Viktor looked over at Svetlana.

'Very well', she said. 'But be careful not to kick the ball in his face. He's very sensitive.'

I used to think I was a wimpy vampire, but I've got nothing on Viktor. Who ever heard of a vampire who's scared of footballs? Cricket stumps, I could understand, but not footballs.

THURSDAY 9TH JANUARY

I was pleased to have Viktor in the game at first. I'm so used to being the worst player it was great to have someone who got the ball even less than me.

It's not that Viktor was terrible. He was much better than a human, though that's not saying much. It's just that we have some really brilliant players here. The scores after ninety minutes are usually things like 347 to 256, because we all dart around with full vampire speed.

About twenty minutes in, Viktor fell to the floor, grasped his calf and started crying. We don't really have any rules about fouls in vampire football. None of us feel physical pain, so we don't usually bother. There have been a couple of times when players' legs have been broken and we've had to stop the game while they healed, but Viktor didn't seem badly injured.

I thought we'd better let him take a penalty just to stop him sobbing. I called everyone to a halt and set the ball in front of goal.

Viktor took a run up and kicked the ball between the two capes we were using as posts. Mike was in goal, and had no problem batting it back.

Viktor grabbed the ball with his hands, dumped it on the other side of the capes and ran around cheering.

I'm not quite sure what he was trying to do. Maybe he thought he could trick us with his vampire speed. It was all rather embarrassing.

When we refused to let the goal stand, Viktor punctured the ball with one of his fangs, stamped on it and stormed off.

'Amazing the kind of idiots they let into the coven these days, isn't it?' asked Mike.

'I know,' I said. 'Unbelievable.'

Friday 10th January

I sat next to Lenora in class today, which was very distracting. Obviously, all vampires are meant to have supernatural beauty, as it helps us seduce prey. It doesn't usually work on me, because I know it's just a trick to get blood. But I think Lenora is gorgeous. She's a total vamp, as we say. She has black hair, dark eyes and thin lips that seem to be constantly turned into a cruel sneer. Or maybe that's just when I'm around.

I noticed she had a book with her, so I asked what it was. She said it was called *A Tale of Two Cities*, but I was probably too young to remember it.

I wish she'd stop going on about my age. She was turned into a vampire when she was fifteen, just like I was. So what if it happened a few decades earlier? It's the transformation age that counts. Everyone knows that.

The Wimpy Vampire Strikes Back

Saturday 11th January

I tried reading *A Tale of Two Cities* this morning so I could chat to Lenora about it. Unfortunately there were loads of bits about guillotines, and it made me too thirsty to concentrate.

I searched all around the castle for a book about the Victorian age, so I could impress her with my knowledge of her era. Eventually I found one in my sister's room that was full of cartoons and quizzes.

It didn't make me wish I'd been born fifty years earlier. I thought I'd had it tough living through two world wars and fifty-seven Eurovision Song Contests, but things were even worse back then.

The Wimpy Vampire Strikes Back

Cecil came round tonight to moan about the lack of cobwebs on the stairwell. He said that spider webs are traditional and without them we might as well be walking around a shopping mall.

'Uncleanliness is next to ungodliness', he said, slamming the door.

I don't know why he was making such a fuss. The stairs still work, don't they? They get him from one floor to another. What more does he want?

I went down to Mrs Dean's room to pass on the comment. She said she was too busy to do the stairs, though I noticed she'd

had plenty of time to do her own room. There were cobwebs dangling down from all the corners, and a thick layer of dust on the floorboards.

Then Mrs Dean accused me of trying to overwork her. I wasn't trying to do anything. I was just relating Cecil's complaint. I wish they'd rant at each other instead of going through me.

SUNDAY 12TH JANUARY

I sat next to Lenora again today. While we were supposed to be copying notes from the blackboard, I told her some of the facts I'd learned about the filthy slums, stinky diseases and overcrowded prisons of Victorian Britain.

'What would you know about it?' she asked. 'You weren't even alive.'

'I've read a book about it,' I said.

'Well, doesn't that just make you the expert?' she asked. 'What would I know? I only lived through it.'

'Sorry,' I said. 'I was just trying to take an interest.'

'Well, don't,' she said. 'I'm sick and tired of everyone going on about how awful the nineteenth century was. I had a wonderful time, if you must know. I had a steady supply of fresh blood in the orphanage near where we lived...'

She used to feed off the blood of orphans? That's disgusting! She's a fiend! She's a monster! She's a savage! She's a...

No, it's no use. I still fancy her.

The Wimpy Vampire Strikes Back

MONDAY 13TH JANUARY

A mist drifted over the island early this morning, so I went down to the graveyard next to the castle for a brood. I was really looking forward to moping about my doomed love for Lenora. It's been a couple of years since I've been able to wallow in romantic failure, and I couldn't wait to get started.

When I got to the graveyard I found that it was already full. I should have known. You have to get there really early to get a spot on misty days. Contrary to popular misconceptions, vampires can go out in daylight, but we much prefer freezing, gloomy, damp and drizzly conditions. If there's a bitter wind too, that's a bonus.

I tramped round for ages looking for a spare grave. I eventually spotted a nice crumbly stone with a towel stretched under it. I tried sitting there, but a vampire called Hans leant across from the next grave.

'Excuse me, but my good friend Eddie is sitting there', he said in his thick Bavarian accent. 'He shall return shortly.'

I sighed and got back to my feet.

On my way back to the castle, I spotted my sister leaning against one of the graves. I asked her what she was

brooding about, and she said that Mum and Dad wouldn't let her go to see Lady Gaga live on the mainland because it was too expensive.

What a complete and utter waste of a brooding space. I was all set to torture myself with the inevitability of eternal loneliness, and she was wasting a spot fretting about excessive booking fees.

Mrs Dean changed the soil in my coffin while I was out. She's supposed to do it every couple of weeks, but she hasn't done mine since last autumn. It looks much more inviting with all that fresh soil. I think I might get in right now and have a brood, in fact. Here goes...

Why do the girls I fancy never fancy me? Why am I doomed to spend eternity alone? Why? Why? Why?

10PM

I had a lovely brood, but now it's time for me to stop moping and take charge of my life. Tomorrow I'm going to ask Lenora out. As long as I wear a nice cape and get down on one knee like vampires did in her day, there's no way she'll be able to refuse.

11PM

Who am I kidding? She used to drink the blood of orphans. As if she'd have any qualms about breaking the heart of an undead dweeb like me.

The Wimpy Vampire Strikes Back

TUESDAY 14TH JANUARY

I finally got round to writing my report about the Seth incident tonight. I couldn't go into much detail about how stupid Mum, Dad and Cecil were, because it would mean I'd have to choose a new Circle of Elders. But I enjoyed describing how my quick thinking saved the day.

I'm still over thirty reports behind, but at least that's one I can tick off my list.

The Wimpy Vampire Strikes Back

By the time I'd emailed it to the Vampire Council and made my way down to the kitchen, I'd missed all the blood. I had to scrape the congealed dregs from the bottom of the barrels and they were hard, clotted and disgusting. It was like eating the bogies of someone who's just had a nosebleed.

I'm sick of this. I should have the thickest, tastiest type O- delivered to my room whenever I please. I should have the finest, crumbliest, mossiest grave reserved for me at all times. And I should be treated with respect by sexy female vampires.

Maybe I'll just quit. Mum, Dad or Cecil can take over if they like. They're incompetent, but how much harm can they really do? We're on decent terms with the werewolf community now, so they're unlikely to attack. The blood collection squad are good at keeping a low profile, so I doubt we'll be traced by any vampire slayers.

The Vampire Council will probably be unhappy if I resign so soon, but I don't care. If they can't be bothered replying to my email, I don't see why I should worry what they think.

WEDNESDAY 15TH JANUARY

I had crèche duty today. The crèche is in a small room at the back of the minus third floor we set up for three babies called Nimrod, Nathaniel and Zylphina.

Vampire babies shouldn't exist at all, of course. Humans are only transformed if we deliberately mix blood with them.

The Wimpy Vampire Strikes Back

Vampire blood has to flow into an open human vein for ages, so it's unlikely to happen by accident.

It's also unlikely that anyone would transform a baby on purpose. They're never going to grow up, so what's the point? Nonetheless, every now and then some misguided fool creates one, and it's up to covens to take them in.

My sister was obsessed with the babies when we first got here, and even did some of my shifts for me. But all it took was for Nathaniel to burp blood down her pink dress for the novelty to wear off.

Crèche duty can be boring, but it's not too difficult. All you have to do is fill their blood bottles from the barrel in the corner, make sure they don't get out of their coffin-shaped cots, and pick them up if they start crying.

They seemed quiet today, so I played *Angry Birds* on my phone to pass the time. When I looked up, Nimrod's cot was empty.

The Wimpy Vampire Strikes Back

I sprung to my feet and searched around the room. There was a basket of blood-stained baby grows in the corner, but he wasn't under those. The top of the barrel in the corner was missing, but he wasn't bobbing around inside. It looked like he'd been in, though. There were tiny foot- and handprints all around it.

I heard laughter above me and looked up to see Nimrod jumping down from the wardrobe with the lid of the barrel in his hand. He landed on my chest and banged the lid into my face over and over again.

I couldn't believe how much energy he had. No wonder you're not supposed to feed them more than two bottles a day. Even when I'd thrown him to the floor, he crawled around my ankles, nipping at them with his tiny fangs.

I don't know what good he thought that would do. Vampires can't survive on vampire blood. Our lives would be much, much simpler if we could.

By the time my shift ended, Nimrod was still leaping around, and Nathanial and Zylphina were bawling their eyes out. Luckily it was Cecil's shift next. I couldn't have wished it on a nicer vampire.

Thursday 16th January

Sometimes problems work themselves out. This morning I went down to the archive room to file a meeting report.

The archive room is a dusty vault at the end of the minus fourth floor. To get there, you have to walk down a corridor lit by flickering torches and creak open a steel door. It seems a waste to use such a brilliant room for fusty old files and books. Most vampires would bite your neck off for a room like that.

When I got there today I heard shuffling from behind one of the tall wooden shelves.

'Out!' I shouted. 'I shouldn't have to keep telling you'.

I'd caught my sister and her friends Amber and Ellie practising a dance routine down there a few months ago, and I assumed they were at it again.

I walked over to the shelf, expecting to see the girls flailing around. Instead I found Svetlana holding the leather-bound coven record book while Viktor peered over her arm.

'Sorry,' I said.

The Wimpy Vampire Strikes Back

'You should be', said Svetlana, scowling at me. 'You can't just overthrow the head of a coven and put yourself in their place.'

'I didn't overthrow anyone', I said. 'Someone suggested I take over and I agreed.'

'A likely story', she said, tapping the book. 'And I suppose you've never read your own record book. And you've no idea this coven should be rightfully ruled by the Carpathian family. And that the natural heir is not you but my son Viktor!'

Viktor jumped out, holding up his fists and skipping back

and forth. 'I hereby challenge you to a duel in accordance with ancient vampire law!' he shouted.

I wouldn't have minded fighting a duel against him. Of all the vampires in the coven, he's the one I'd be most likely to beat. And that would make me look pretty cool in front of Lenora. But what would be the point of battling for something I didn't even want?

'Hang on a minute', I said. 'How do you know I'm not prepared to negotiate?'

'My son will never share power!' said Svetlana.

'He might not have to', I said. 'Maybe if you agree to my terms I'd let you take over right away. For example, you could make sure a flask of fresh blood is left outside my room every morning so I don't have to queue with the others. And you could make sure one of the best graves is reserved for me.'

'Really?' she asked. 'That's all you want to hand over power?'

I probably should have held out for two flasks a day.

Friday 17th January

I arranged a meeting between Viktor, Svetlana and the Circle of Elders this evening. Mum, Dad and Cecil were mad when I announced I was handing over power. But when Svetlana assured them their positions were safe they seemed to calm down.

Cecil pretended he'd wanted to track down the rightful leader of the coven all along, which I took as my cue to leave.

The Wimpy Vampire Strikes Back

I told Viktor he was responsible for writing meeting reports and left them to their pointless discussions.

I can't believe I'm finally free! No more paperwork about petty squabbles for me!

I found a lovely flask of blood waiting outside my room, just as requested. Even better, dark storm clouds were looming over the island. I rushed outside and saw that one of the graves at the front had a new stone...

RESERVED FOR Nigel Mullet

I leant against it and unscrewed my flask. I couldn't believe I had my own private grave. Now I could finally rest in peace, aptly enough. The only other vampire with a reserved plot is

Seth, who's built a pyramid on the edge of the graveyard. Apparently that's how they used to bury people back in his day, so it makes him feel at home.

'Reserving graves is unfair!' shouted Hans from a few graves back.

I didn't even bother pointing out the hypocrisy of this. I just stared out at the sea as the clouds broke and icy rain pelted down. It was perfect. The only problem was I was so happy I couldn't brood properly.

SATURDAY 18TH JANUARY

Word must have spread about Viktor taking over because everyone keeps asking me about him. Rob, Mike and Henry even said they wished I'd stayed in charge. I didn't notice any of them congratulating me on doing a good job while I was leader.

Mr Dashwood gave us a lesson about the Vampire – Werewolf war at school this morning. I've seen a battle between vampires and werewolves, and it was pretty exciting, so you'd think an entire war would be the most awesome thing ever. But you wouldn't know from Mr Dashwood's wittering. All he did was point out places on an ancient yellow map and make us write down the names of the most famous battles. He might as well have been talking about the history of the sewage system for all the drama he injected into it.

Halfway through, he went out to collect another map from his study and Seth ran over to my desk to ask what was going

The Wimpy Vampire Strikes Back

on with Viktor. I was about to tell him I'd handed over power because I couldn't be bothered leading the coven, when I noticed Lenora coming over too.

She seemed interested in what I had to say for once, so I thought I'd make myself sound more heroic. I said I'd fought fang and nail to stop Viktor from taking over my beloved coven, but I was overruled by the Circle of Elders.

The whole class were gathered around my desk by the time Mr Dashwood came in clutching a faded map. I tried to explain that it wasn't my fault, but that didn't stop him calling me up to the front.

When he started fumbling around in his drawer, I thought he was looking for his holy water, but he went straight for the punishment box! I can't believe I got crucifixed just because everyone was talking to me.

I tried really hard not to react as he opened the box. But it

only took a glimpse of the tiny silver Jesus hanging from the cross to send me howling to the floor with my head in my hands. I rolled around and sobbed, desperate for the sharp ache behind my eyes to die down.

I can't believe I did that in front of Lenora. She must think I'm such a loser.

Sunday 19th January

Seth came round to my room tonight to apologize. I told him it was Mr Dashwood's fault for overreacting, and invited him in to play *Need for Speed* to show there were no hard feelings.

Driving games are usually much better with two players, but I don't think Seth really understood what was going on. He kept crashing into barriers and driving the wrong way. It's not surprising, really. He's been in this coven for over a hundred years. He's probably never even seen a car. I told him to imagine he was driving a chariot, but he just lifted his hand in the air and did a whipping mime.

After a while, he ran off to fetch a game from his room. I was hoping it might be the new *Call of Duty*, but it turned out to be an ancient board game where you had to throw sticks and move counters around.

It was pretty dull. I couldn't really see the point in faffing around with a 3,000-year-old game when I had a pile of new videogames and a HD TV in front of me, but I tried my best.

It was a great example of vampire tolerance when you think

47

about it. Most humans can't even get on with those from other nations, yet there I was making friends with someone from another era. If I didn't need to drain the blood of innocent humans to survive, I'd be a model of understanding and decency.

MONDAY 20TH JANUARY

It was raining heavily tonight, so I popped down to my grave for a good mope. When I got there I found Cecil sitting in my spot and staring out at the sea.

I coughed and pointed to the headstone.

He said that my sister had been using the grave this evening when she'd heard ghostly wailing voices, so she'd sent him out to investigate. He hadn't discovered anything yet, but was hanging around to make sure.

Well, excuse me. I thought the stone said, 'Reserved for Nigel Mullet'. I didn't realize it actually said, 'Reserved for Nigel Mullet and any freeloading hangers-on who want to sit here.'

Cecil wouldn't budge so I had to traipse around looking for another spot. The only free grave was right at the back. There was no lichen or moss on the stone, you couldn't see the ocean and Hans was on the grave next to it playing soft rock on his old-fashioned cassette player. I wouldn't have minded if he'd been playing funeral dirges or Radiohead, but how are you supposed to brood to Bon Jovi?

After a few minutes I gave up and went back to my room.

The Wimpy Vampire Strikes Back

TUESDAY 21st JANUARY

Everyone is on strict rations of half a pint a day because
Viktor has fallen out with Mike and Rob. Apparently he
called them 'a pair of smelly plebs who need to learn their
place'. Now they're refusing to harvest any blood until he
apologizes and we're all going to have to make do with the
stuff Henry collects.

The Wimpy Vampire Strikes Back

I suppose I should try to sort it out. The problem is, my private blood supply doesn't seem to have been affected, and I don't want to rock the boat. I know it sounds selfish, but it's important I drink enough to stay alert in these difficult times. In a way, keeping quiet to protect my daily blood delivery is the least selfish thing I can do.

11PM

I went round to see Seth tonight and he showed me how he puts his make-up on. Both men and women used to wear it back in his time, and he saw no reason to give up after he transformed.

He uses this black dust called kohl to trace almond shapes around his eyes. Then he dabs rouge on his cheeks, paints his nails with henna and rubs scented oil on his neck. Most vampires would have found this weird, but I didn't because I'm open-minded and understanding.

Seth offered to apply the make-up to my face, and I was reluctant at first. But when he said it would help to ward off evil, I thought I might as well give it a try.

I thought I looked quite cool when he was finished, and I gazed in the mirror, imagining myself riding chariots, building pyramids and bathing in milk (yes, we vampires can see ourselves in mirrors; don't believe *everything* you see in horror flicks).

I'd forgotten all about it by the time I went back down to my room. I passed Dad and Cecil on the stairwell, and I couldn't

understand why they were scowling.

'I told you something like this would happen', said Cecil. 'You were too soft on him, and you've got no one but yourself to blame'.

Dad just shook his head. I wonder what he wants sometimes. He complains I don't have enough friends, but when I make them he's still not happy.

WEDNESDAY 22ND JANUARY

Everyone was really tired in class today. Even Mr Dashwood didn't have the energy to tell anyone off. I got my phone out and played *Angry Birds* in the middle of his lecture about anti-vampire weaponry and he didn't even mention it. He just kept droning on about religious symbol barricades and holy water traps.

After the lesson, I caught up with Lenora in the corridor.

'What about these rations?' I asked, faking a yawn. 'They're a real fang in the neck, aren't they?'

'They're a disgrace', she said. 'I can't believe you handed over power to that twerp.'

'Don't think I went down without a fight', I said. 'You should have seen me in there. It was like something from the Vampire–Werewolf war.'

'Well, I hope someone does something', she said. 'Half a pint a day isn't enough.'

I glanced around. Most of the others were strolling listlessly away, so I leaned in and whispered, 'If you're really thirsty, you could pop over to my room. I've got a couple of spare flasks I could be persuaded to share.'

Lenora grinned at me. I caught a brief glimpse of fang, which shows how thirsty these rations must be making her.

'Sounds good', she said. 'Maybe I'll see you later.'

I'm much better at talking to girls now. Just a couple of years ago, I'd have taken ages to work up the courage to ask her round for a drink. This time I just came right out with it. I'll probably get a snog out of it, too. I'm as smooth as a glass of type A– these days.

The Wimpy Vampire Strikes Back

THURSDAY 23RD JANUARY

Lenora knocked on my door at four this morning.

'Can I come in?' she whispered.

I switched off my PlayStation, selected some romantic piano music on iTunes, gave my fangs a quick brush, took a couple of wine glasses out of my cupboard and lit my candelabra.

'Come in', I said. I was going to say, 'Enter my realm', but I didn't want to overdo it.

Lenora threw the door open. She was wearing a black dress that tapered to a thin waist and a wide-brimmed hat with a green feather on the front.

'Is that offer of a drink still on?' she asked.

'Of course', I said, gesturing to the two glasses.

'Great', she said. 'Come in guys'.

The Wimpy Vampire Strikes Back

She stepped inside, followed by Ezekiel and Abraham, two middle-aged vampires with brushy moustaches, stovepipe hats and velvet-lined capes.

I sighed and rooted around in my cupboard for two more glasses.

Ezekiel and Abraham are so boring. They spent all night talking about something called 'the Corn Laws'. I'm sure I would have fallen asleep if that were possible.

Lenora nodded and smiled as if it was the most fascinating

thing she'd ever heard. I bet she wasn't interested either. She just wanted to make a big deal out of being older than me.

When Lenora's friends had drained my blood and my will to live, they bowed and took their leave. I was hoping she'd stay behind, but she curtseyed and left with them.

Friday 24th January

I can't believe I gave up two entire blood flasks for a curtsey. So much for the snog I was hoping for!

That's what I get for fancying a Victorian vampire, I suppose. She'll probably want me to propose to her before I'm even allowed to hold her hand.

I wish I fancied a vampire from an era when everyone was less uptight, like the 1960s or cavemen days.

Why do I always have to make it difficult for myself? Am I destined to spend eternity alone?

Hang on a minute, I feel a brood coming on. Better nip down to the graveyard before someone steals my place.

Saturday 25th January

Lenora's stupid friends obviously can't keep their mouths shut. Shortly after I took in my blood flask this morning, I got a knock on the door.

It was Rob from the blood collection squad.

'All right, mate?' he said. 'I heard you had a stash tucked away in there.'

The Wimpy Vampire Strikes Back

I could hardly refuse him a sip after all the work he's done, but I was still annoyed that word about my supply had spread.

Ten minutes later, a French vampire called Arnaud called round to see if I could spare a glass of the delicious stuff he'd heard so much about. I have no idea why I let him in.

'Excellent consistency,' he said, holding the glass up to my candle and swirling the blood round. He stuck his beaky nose into the glass and gave it a loud sniff. 'I'm getting sugar... I'm getting iron... hints of copper... '

He took a swig of the blood, swilled it round his mouth and swallowed it. 'Excellent!'

By the time I got rid of the pretentious fiend, there was a massive queue outside my door. There was even an

argument going on halfway down the line, because Hans had reserved a place for Eddy.

I brought out my flask and let everyone have a sip. When it was finished, I told them my supply was over, and that they should never ever come back to check if I had more.

I'm going to have to bring my flasks in right away and hide them behind my coffin from now on, and it's all because of those loud-mouthed Victorians.

SUNDAY 26TH JANUARY

Today we had a geography lesson about vampire covens around the world. The main ones are in Russia, Alaska, Canada and Finland. There used to be a huge one in Antarctica, but that's been abandoned due to melting ice caps.

I wonder if all those humans who drive gas-guzzling cars would feel guilty if they knew they'd destroyed our natural habitat.

Probably not. We get such a bad portrayal in the media that they might even be pleased. Whenever you see a vampire on telly, they're always running after some young girl so they can drink her blood. In reality, that's a very small part of what we do. But we still get landed with the stereotypes.

Seth got told off halfway through the lesson for doodling. I looked over at his scroll and saw he was actually writing hieroglyphics.

The Wimpy Vampire Strikes Back

I was going to stick up for him, but I didn't want to get crucifixed again.

Not that Mr Dashwood looked like he had the energy to punish anyone. He just told Seth to stop and went back to yakking on about covens.

11PM

Football tonight. Everyone was really weak because of the rationing, so for once I was the best player on the pitch. I scored sixty goals in the first half, but Mike asked where I was getting my energy from, so I dialled it down. The last thing I want is for everyone to work out that my blood supply isn't really finished.

The other team had Ron in goal, so they didn't have much of a chance. Ron's legs were severed in a motorbike accident in the seventies. For some reason, he held them the wrong way round while they were healing, so now he has backwards legs.

He could chop them off and heal them on the right way round again, but he says he likes being different. And yet he moans when he's last to be picked.

Luckily, the other team got him tonight. Every time he tried to run forward to catch the ball, his legs went the wrong way and he got tangled in the net. It was actually quite hard to avoid scoring against him.

The Wimpy Vampire Strikes Back

MONDAY 27th JANUARY

Incredibly, things have got even worse. Apparently, Viktor
called Henry a 'rapscallion' and now he's refusing to fetch blood
too. I'm not sure what's so offensive about that. Maybe it was
a more serious insult back in his day.

I thought I was a bad leader, but the speed at which
Viktor has brought the coven to a standstill is unbelievable.
I don't even know what's going to happen to us now.
Vampires don't die without blood, but we eventually
become too thin and weak to move. In a couple of months
this coven will probably look like the supermodels section
in a wax museum.

We can't let it come to that. Someone has to stand up to
Viktor. It should be me. But my daily flasks are still turning up,

The Wimpy Vampire Strikes Back

so I might leave it for now. But I promise I'll confront him the moment everyone else is too weak to move or speak.

TUESDAY 28TH JANUARY

Lenora came round to my room again tonight. And this time she didn't bring her boring friends with her. I got a flask out from behind my coffin and pretended it was the last of my supply.

I poured her a glass and we sat on my coffin and had a good chat. She seems to be warming to me, hopefully not just because of the blood.

She told me all about her old coven in the East End of London. They managed to keep themselves secret until one of their members went on a killing spree in 1888 and they had to disband. Luckily, the papers blamed it all on someone called 'Jack the Ripper', so they were never tracked down.

Lenora seemed interested to hear about my old life as well. I told her about how I used to trade in my old PlayStation titles at Games Exchange to get money off new ones. Actually, she might not have been that fascinated, because she kept looking out the window. I suppose it wouldn't have meant much to her if she doesn't know what a computer game is, but it's still got to be more interesting than the Corn Laws.

'Freshen your blood?' I asked.

I poured her another glass and sneaked closer. I knew it was a good time to try for a snog, but I couldn't make myself do it. Maybe if I'd had a couple more glasses.

'I'm glad you saved this blood', she said. 'It means you'll still have the energy to confront Viktor.'

'Yeah', I said, inching closer.

'Excellent', said Lenora, leaping up. 'I knew you'd do it! Get him to apologize to Rob, Mike and Henry, so we can resolve this stupid situation.'

She blew me a kiss and walked out. I suppose a blown kiss is a step up from a curtsey, but I can't believe I wasted such a brilliant chance for a snog. And now I've got to confront Viktor and put my precious blood supply at risk. I don't know why I bother with girls.

The Wimpy Vampire Strikes Back

WEDNESDAY 29TH JANUARY

Viktor and Svetlana weren't in their room today, so I went up to the discussion room.

I knocked on the door and a vampire I'd never seen before answered. He was over six feet tall and had long blond hair and sunglasses. He was wearing a black sweatshirt and had a leather holster around his waist.

'Yes?' he asked.

'I was just wondering if Viktor and Svetlana are around', I replied.

He swung the door open and beckoned me in. Svetlana was sitting at the far end of the table. Viktor was on her knee, sucking blood from a bottle. Six other vampires were standing behind her. They looked almost identical to the one who let me in, with long blond hair, sunglasses and holsters.

'Meet the new blood collection squad', she said. 'They've already brought in an excellent crop'.

Svetlana pointed at the table, where three barrels of blood, a ladle and a set of wine glasses were set out. 'Try it'.

I picked up a glass and went through the barrels one by one.

They were all utterly, utterly amazing. Last time I drank blood that fresh and delicious I was sucking it from an open vein.

The first barrel was a salty type A−, as thin and smooth as tomato juice. The second was a tangy, peppery type B+, the sort

of thing I'd dip nachos into if I ate food. The third was a thick, sweet type AB I, a kind of red custard.

I drained the last glass, realizing that I'd just enjoyed the finest three-course meal of my vampire life.

'So what did you want to see us about?' asked Svetlana.

I was so distracted by the quality of the blood it took me a while to remember.

'Sorry,' I said. 'I was wondering if Viktor could apologize to Rob, Mike and Henry.'

'And why on earth would he want to do that?' asked Svetlana.

'So they can start collecting blood from the mainland again,' I said.

'But we have a new blood collection squad now,' said

Svetlana. 'And I think you'll agree they're doing a much better job.'

I ran my tongue over my fangs. The taste of the sweet AB+ was still on them. She wasn't wrong.

Viktor took the bottle out of his mouth. 'I hate those smelly old vampires! Don't ever mention them again!'

'The king has spoken,' said Svetlana. 'And if you want any more of this premium-quality blood, I suggest you listen.'

I looked down at the barrels. My fangs were extending again, even though I'd just fed. I was shocked at my own greed.

THURSDAY 30TH JANUARY

There's a large speedboat moored to some rocks at the back of the island. It has a cabin with mirrored windows and a large deck at the back.

This must be the boat the blond vampires arrived in. It would certainly explain how they can get the blood here while it's still fresh.

There was a flask of that gorgeous sweet AB+ waiting outside my room when I got back. I glugged it right down, and it was just as delicious as I remembered.

The Wimpy Vampire Strikes Back

I expected the rations to have been lifted by now, but no one seems to have announced anything. Cecil was on kitchen duty, and he was still only letting people take half a pint from the barrel. Judging by the smell, he was still serving the stale old leftovers of Henry's last trip to the mainland.

When Lenora asked me how my meeting had gone, I said it was fine and everything would be back to normal soon. Which might be true for all I know.

Friday 31st January

I'm getting a little worried about this whole Viktor situation. I don't like the look of those blond vampires, I don't like the way he isn't sharing the new blood, and I certainly don't like the way Svetlana referred to him as 'the king'.

This evening I went to talk to my parents about it.

When I got to their room, I found Dad blasting out a violin concerto on his ancient record player, while Mum and Cecil were dancing in the middle of the floor. Needless to say, there were a couple of empty barrels lying around.

I couldn't believe it. They'd been drinking too much, they'd been neglecting their duties, and, worst of all, they'd been getting more of that lovely blood than me. I knew I should have asked for more.

'I came here to ask you what you thought about Viktor,' I said. 'But I can see you're busy so I'll call back tomorrow.'

Mum staggered over and draped her arm around my

shoulder. 'Viktor's not so bad', she slurred. 'He's like you. A bit wet, but all right really.'

I hadn't called round to be insulted by family members, but I thought I might as well keep trying.

'How has he been behaving in Circle of Elders meetings?' I asked.

'He's cancelled those', said Mum. She hiccupped blood down her chin. 'But who needs boring meetings when you've got lovely fresh stuff like this?'

She flung her arm in the direction of the table, knocking her glass to the floor.

'And blood's more important than your duty to the coven, is it?' I asked.

'Yes,' said Cecil. 'Have you tasted this stuff? It's amazing. There's a salty flavour, a spicy flavour, a sweet flavour...'
I slammed the door and stomped back to my room. I couldn't believe they'd betray the coven just for a few swigs. I hope it tastes like ashes in their mouths.

When I got back to my room, I noticed that Viktor's guards had delivered another flask of blood. I thought about taking it up to the discussion room and flinging it in Viktor's stupid face.

'Here's what I think of your bribery,' I'd say as I splashed the liquid all over his little suit.

I thought I'd better take a sip first, to check what flavour it was.

No prizes for guessing I didn't throw it in Viktor's face after all. I quaffed the whole thing down, and it didn't taste like ashes in my mouth. It was delicious – a gloopy type A+ with a sort of honey aftertaste. I can honestly say I've tried nothing like it before. I just hope that French vampire Arnaud doesn't get hold of any. He'd never shut up.

SATURDAY 1ST FEBRUARY

Word seems to have spread about the new blood collection squad. Everyone is convinced it means rationing will be over soon. I don't have the heart to tell them it could be over right now. I wonder when Viktor's going to make an announcement.

Mr Dashwood gave us something he called a 'science lesson' today. It was complete guff, although no one else seemed to mind. They all just copied down his notes, while I looked around in disbelief.

The lesson was about the origin of vampire life, and Mr Dashwood gave us the same old story about how ancient gods married humans and created a new race with special powers. What evidence is there for this? Has Mr Dashwood done a DNA test on himself and found he was 5 per cent god? No, he's just regurgitating the silly folk tales he'd been told.

Say what you like about humans, but at least they bothered to find out where they came from. It wasn't good news, and had something to do with monkeys as far as I can remember, but full marks to them for working it out anyway.

5PM

I just tasted the latest flask from Viktor's squad and it was the best yet. It was a thin type AB− with a strong cinnamon flavour.

The Wimpy Vampire Strikes Back

Every time I think I've found my new favourite, they go ahead and find an even nicer one.

SUNDAY 2ND FEBRUARY

Lenora came over to my desk after school today.

'Rob, Mike and Henry still haven't heard anything from Viktor,' she said. 'Any idea when he's going to give them their jobs back?'

'I don't think he's going to,' I said. 'He's got those blond vampires to fetch blood now.'

Lenora took a handkerchief out of her sleeve and dabbed the corner of her eyes with it. 'I'm sure Rob and Mike will be all right. But the job was really important for Henry's self-esteem. Since he lost his role he's been sitting around his room all day in his long johns. It's terrible to see.'

'I bet it is,' I said.

'Why don't you ask Viktor if those blond vampires could take him along next time they harvest blood?' she asked. 'It would mean ever so much to him.'

'Okay,' I said. 'I'll try my best.'

Why did I promise to do that? Now I've got to grovel to that little snake again.

MONDAY 3RD FEBRUARY

I knocked on Viktor's door and one of the blond vampires showed me in. They'd made so many changes to the room

The Wimpy Vampire Strikes Back

The Wimpy Vampire Strikes Back

I was amazed they'd found the time to gather any blood at all.

The oak table had been chopped up and sculpted into two chairs, which Viktor and Svetlana were sitting on. Svetlana's chair had a long, straight back and narrow armrests. Viktor's had a wide seat and long wooden arms with tiny fang shapes carved in the end. Whoever sculpted them must have been very brave. Carpentry is outlawed by the Health and Safety Division of the Vampire Council due to the risk of

accidental staking. Most vampires feel humiliated and frustrated buying flat-pack furniture, but it's better than risking your life.

'What do you want?' asked Svetlana.

'Could you let Henry join those guys on the blood collection squad?' I asked. 'It would give him a role and help with his self-esteem.'

Viktor scowled at me.

'The king can't concern himself with the emotional wellbeing of every insignificant little serf in the coven,' said Svetlana. 'His example should be enough to inspire them.'

Inspire them to do what? Throw tantrums? Sit on their mummy's laps looking like a satanic ventriloquist's dummy?

'And he does,' I said. 'But there's this girl I fancy, and I sort of promised her I'd sort it all out.'

Svetlana stood up.

'What is our species coming to?' she yelled. 'If you're attracted to a girl you should stalk her like a normal vampire, not bother me with stupid requests.'

'Sorry,' I said. 'Just thought I'd ask.'

'Well, don't bother next time,' she said. 'We've tried being nice. We've given you blood. We've given you a grave. But let me assure you of one thing. If the carrot doesn't work, we shall not be afraid to use the stick.'

Svetlana nodded at one of the blond vampires. He opened the leather holster on his belt ... and drew out a sharp wooden stake!

The Wimpy Vampire Strikes Back

TUESDAY 4TH FEBRUARY

My hands are shaking as I try to write this. I've been lurking in my coffin all day, with my chair shoved up against the door.

You're not allowed to carry stakes! The Vampire Council strictly forbids it. It's pretty much the worst thing you can do, short of vampicide.

I don't even understand why anyone would risk carrying one. If you bumped into a vampire slayer all he'd have to do is overpower you and wallop the horrible thing into your chest.

Then you'd be actually, properly dead. Not dead in the sense of hanging around graveyards and drinking blood, but dead in the sense of never moving or thinking again. Doesn't that frighten those blond bimbos?

It's all well and good to be reckless if you're a vampire. I once forgot to wear my seatbelt for an entire car journey, for example. But those guards are taking it too far.

I need to tell someone. My parents are drinking so much blood at the moment, they won't care. Mr Dashwood would probably crucifix me for lying. Lenora will think I'm a wimp if I go crying to her.

Maybe I should call a coven meeting and announce it to everyone at once. But what if Viktor stakes me to make an example?

The Wimpy Vampire Strikes Back

11PM

Okay. As far as I'm concerned, yesterday didn't happen. I didn't go to the discussion room, I didn't argue with Svetlana and I definitely didn't see a stake. I'm just going to live my life and try to forget about those stupid guards.

I'd better keep my diary in my back pocket from now on. The last thing I need is for those blond vampires to raid my room and find out I've been badmouthing Viktor.

The Wimpy Vampire Strikes Back

Note to Viktor: If you have somehow managed to get hold of this diary, I would like to apologize for the offensive remarks in it. They were written in jest. The truth is, I think you're an excellent king and I hope you rule us for centuries to come.

WEDNESDAY 5TH FEBRUARY

Mr Dashwood gave us a lesson about vampire reproduction today. The subject obviously embarrassed him, and I wondered why he attempted it at all.

I don't know why vampires of Mr Dashwood's generation find reproduction so hard to talk about. None of us would be here if another vampire hadn't mixed their blood with ours. It's not very pleasant, but it's how we all got here, so we might as well be open about it.

Mr Dashwood drew a diagram of some fangs going into a neck on the blackboard, which set off a wave of giggles. Then he dragged a skeleton out of the cupboard and pointed out where all the best veins were. I noticed that Lenora and Seth were looking down at their books and trying not to laugh, so I thought I'd increase the awkwardness factor.

'Sir, can you show us how you'd go about transforming that skeleton if it were a human,' I said.

'Very well,' said Mr Dashwood. 'If it's going to help you learn.'

Mr Dashwood tiptoed up behind the skeleton and pretended to stick his fangs into its neck with a really serious expression on his face.

'Smooth!' I shouted. 'Check out the moves!'

Everyone burst out laughing and Mr Dashwood dragged the skeleton back to the cupboard.

'Right, that's it for today,' he said. 'You're obviously too immature for this lesson. I'll try again when you're older.'

'But we won't get any older,' I said, which made everyone laugh even more.

'I've had enough of your smart mouth,' said Mr Dashwood.

I thought he might holy water me, but I think the embarrassment had exhausted him, as he just sat at the front while everyone filed out.

I wonder what Mr Dashwood used to do for blood before he joined the coven. All vampires are meant to have super-natural beauty to lure prey. It would be an odd sort of human attracted to Mr Dashwood. But odd people bleed too, I suppose.

THURSDAY 6TH FEBRUARY

Small scrolls were left outside everyone's door this morning. They were sealed with red wax with the letter 'V' stamped in.

I thought the stuffy tone of the invite might annoy some vampires, but everyone seemed excited as I wandered down to school this morning.

No wonder they're all looking forward to it so much. They've still been drinking the remains of that blood Henry harvested a

You are cordially invited to a blood feast
at midnight in the throne room
(previously known as the discussion room).

His Majesty Viktor Carpathian
and the
King Mother Svetlana Carpathian
shall be in attendance.

Bring your own glass. Formal attire.

couple of weeks ago. Well, I say 'drinking'. It's probably so clotted now you need a spoon.

I'd better make a big show of feeling refreshed when I sip this new stuff. It won't go down very well if everyone finds out I've been quaffing it for a whole week already.

FRIDAY 7TH FEBRUARY

I joined the queue outside the so-called 'throne room' just before midnight last night. Even the vampires at the back of the queue had their fangs extended, which shows how thirsty everyone was.

Things were pretty weird inside. I think everyone else was too thirsty to notice, but I felt really uncomfortable.

Viktor and Svetlana were sitting on their thrones at the end of the room, with the blond vampires lined up behind them. A huge oil painting of Viktor had been put up on the wall. Either one of those blond vampires is a talented artist, or they brought it with them in their boat. Both possibilities are disturbing.

At the front of the queue, everyone was ladling blood into their glasses, sipping it and filing past Viktor to thank him. No one used to give me a word of thanks when I was in charge. Now they are all fawning over that little twerp. I couldn't believe it.

Most vampires looked genuinely shocked by the quality of the blood. Ezekiel and Abraham pretty much begged Viktor

The Wimpy Vampire Strikes Back

for another helping, but he pointed them to the back of the queue.

Arnaud was a couple of places in front of me. He did his usual thing of swishing the blood round in the glass and holding it up to the light, but when he tasted it he was lost for words. He just stared at his empty glass with tears running down his face.

When I got to the front, I downed my blood and let out a long sigh of relief. I wasn't even exaggerating that much. The blood was thin and bitter with a sort of citrus taste. It reminded me of the lemonade I used to drink when I was a human.

I thanked Viktor and went straight to the back of the queue. This was partly so no one would suspect I had a private supply and partly because I was desperate for more of the delicious blood.

SATURDAY 8TH FEBRUARY

According to a note in the kitchen, the rationing is still in place, but Viktor will hold blood feasts whenever he can to reward the coven for its patience. He's only doing this so everyone associates him with the taste of that lovely blood. Vampires are as gullible as humans sometimes.

I went round to my parents' room to see if they'd found the blood feast a bit weird too.

Dad and Cecil were sitting around their table and draining one of their barrels.

'Nothing wrong with blood feasts', said Cecil. 'That's how we used to feed all the time when I was a young vampire. There was none of this hiding in your room and sipping your blood in front of the TV back then.'

I can't believe he managed to turn it into an attack on me so quickly.

'That might be true', I said. 'But don't you find it a little

The Wimpy Vampire Strikes Back

strange that he sits on a throne while we all file past and thank him?'

'It's tradition', said Cecil. 'You young vampires would do well to learn about it.'

I realized I wasn't going to get any sense out of them, so I went down to my sister's room to see Mum.

Mum looks after my sister and her friends Amber and Ellie in the daytime when the rest of us are at school. Mr Dashwood decided they were too young for his class, so Mum has to keep them amused with activities like drawing, reading and gluing glitter on stuff.

They're so stupid she could probably keep them entertained

by waving a piece of tinsel up and down all day, but it's good that she makes the effort.

I thought I was imagining things when I opened the door today.

My sister had taken down all her pop and animals posters and replaced them with crudely drawn pictures of Viktor. She was sitting at the table with Amber and Ellie and Mum was helping them trace big red hearts around more scrawled portraits.

'What do you think?' asked Mum.

I turned around and walked straight out again. I didn't want to waste any time engaging with my brainless little sister. Viktor is a dangerous, psychopathic little runt, not a TV talent contest winner. If she had even the slightest bit of intelligence, she'd be working out how to stop him, not creating inept sparkly tributes.

SUNDAY 9TH FEBRUARY

It wasn't just me. I spoke to Lenora after school and she found the blood feast weird too. That proves we've got loads in common.

Lenora said she'd been in the queue when Svetlana had insisted everyone thanked Viktor. Cecil had been at the front, and he'd got the ball rolling with flowery praise.

I can't believe everyone agreed so readily. The whole point of a vampire coven is that we're all equal. We're all strong,

The Wimpy Vampire Strikes Back

we're all fast and we all have supernatural beauty (except perhaps Mr Dashwood). We don't need a king because we're all kings.

I told Lenora I'd have a word with Viktor about the feasts. Then I remembered the stake and wished I hadn't said anything.

Lenora said it would also be great if I could think of a new job for Henry. At least that won't involve the stress of visiting Viktor.

MONDAY 10TH FEBRUARY

This afternoon I stole the skeleton from Mr Dashwood's room and told Henry to bury it in my grave. When he was done, I told him to dig it up again. Now all I have to do is keep

repeating this and I've created a job and done my bit for the vampire economy.

Henry seems to be enjoying himself so far. No doubt it takes him back to his old bodysnatching days. I might even make some fake money to pay him with.

It means I won't be able to use my spot in the graveyard any more, but I don't mind. At least my freeloading family won't be able to use it either.

TUESDAY 11TH FEBRUARY

Lenora caught up with me after school today.

'Thanks for finding a job for Henry,' she said. 'You've really given him his dignity back.'

'Brilliant,' I said. I wasn't sure how much dignity he'd get from burying and digging up the same skeleton over and over again, but I was happy to have helped.

'How did your chat with Viktor go?' she asked.

I was hoping she'd forgotten about that.

'It was all right,' I said. 'But he wants to keep the blood feasts the same for the time being. He says it's the way he's always done things and you know how vampires are about tradition.'

'Okay,' she said. 'Let's have a think about our next move.'

I have no idea what she meant by 'next move'. If it involves her coming round to my room for a snog, I'm all for it. But if it involves me confronting some armed and dangerous vampires, I'm not so keen. I think I can guess which it's going to be.

The Wimpy Vampire Strikes Back

WEDNESDAY 12TH FEBRUARY

My sister was wandering around with the word 'Viktie'
scrawled on her shirt in pen today. I asked her what it meant
and she said that the 'Vikties' are a fan group she's formed with
Amber and Ellie. Apparently, they meet up every day and talk
about their love for Viktor.

'It must be so exciting for you', I said. 'I wonder what sort of
sigh he's going to do next? How do you think he's going to slouch
this time?'

'You're just jealous because he got voted in and you got
voted out', said my sister.

Voted out of what? Nobody voted for anything. I handed
over power.

Before I could say anything, my sister skipped away,
chanting: 'No votes for Nigel! Victory for Viktor!'

This is what she does. She says things that are so wrong
I don't know where to start and then she wanders away as if
she's won. I'll have no sympathy at all if she gets staked by
Viktor's guards.

THURSDAY 13TH FEBRUARY

We had a maths lesson today. Mr Dashwood wrote a list of long
division questions on the blackboard and told us to work
through them. I soon found myself staring out of the window.

'You won't find the answer out there', said Mr Dashwood.

I turned back to the blackboard and sighed.

'I'm sorry to see this is all such an effort for you', said Mr Dashwood. 'Perhaps you think you don't need this lesson.'

'I don't, as a matter of fact', I said. 'I can understand why we need to know history and geography and reproduction, but what use is maths?'

Mr Dashwood smirked. He obviously thought he had a killer comeback lined up.

'Well, let me ask you this', he said. 'If you had a barrel of blood with a diameter of two feet and a height of three feet, and you had ten vampires to feed, how much would you give each of them?'

'I'd probably just give them half a pint each and keep the rest for myself like Viktor does', I said.

There was a gasp from the other pupils. Mr Dashwood stared at me for a moment. I wondered if he was going to crucifix me, but for once he didn't seem very angry.

'That's as maybe', he said. 'But this is a maths lesson, not a politics one.'

I can't believe I got away with that. I was expecting to get holy watered at the very least.

FRIDAY 14TH FEBRUARY

Lenora came over to my desk today and whispered, 'Meet me on the beach at midnight.' She walked out of the room without saying anything more.

I was supposed to do my maths homework this afternoon,

but all I could think about was Lenora's mysterious invitation. The beach is on the east of the island at the bottom of a hill, so no one will be able to see us there. Could it be that Lenora wants to snog me, but needs to be sure her Victorian friends like Ezekiel and Abraham won't see?

I told myself that I was imagining it, that Lenora was from an era when women never made the first move. But then I looked at my calendar. Today is Valentine's Day. That can't be coincidence, can it?

I've got to go now. It's almost eleven, so I've only got an hour to make sure my fangs are totally clean.

SATURDAY 15TH FEBRUARY

I put a clean T-shirt and pair of jeans on

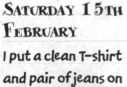

The Wimpy Vampire Strikes Back

and made my way down to the beach in time for midnight. As I climbed over the small hill above the beach, wispy clouds shifted to reveal a bright full moon. The conditions were perfect.

Lenora was standing next to the lapping waves in her green ballgown. As I approached, I took my phone out and started playing Beethoven's 'Moonlight Sonata' through the speakers. I thought it might help with the mood.

'I think you can guess what I've called you here for,' said Lenora.

'Of course,' I said, trying to sound commanding. 'Let us begin.'

'We'd better wait until the others get here,' she said.

'Er... others?'

I looked behind and saw Henry making his way down the hill, with Seth and Mr Dashwood following a few feet behind. I hoped she hadn't promised to snog all of us.

When they'd all arrived, Lenora beckoned us close and said,

'Welcome to the first meeting of the Hirta Liberation Front. Do we all hate Viktor?'

'Yes', we said.

'Do we all want to get him off the throne and out of the coven?' asked Lenora.

'Yes', we said.

'And do we all want our rightful leader back?' she asked.

'Yes', said everyone else, turning to look at me.

Brilliant.

SUNDAY 16TH FEBRUARY

I can't believe I turned up at the beach expecting to get a snog and ended up agreeing to fight for something I don't even want. I hate Viktor, but I also hate the idea of taking charge again. Just thinking about all those meeting reports is stressing me out.

I suppose I'd better go along with all this Liberation Front stuff for now, though. Lenora seems to have her heart set on it.

She's asked me to come up with a plan to overthrow Viktor in time for the next meeting. I told her I had loads of maths homework, but she insisted. So much for my plan to spend tonight beating my time trial records on *Need for Speed*.

MONDAY 17TH FEBRUARY

I didn't manage to finish my maths homework in time for today's lesson. I thought Mr Dashwood would let me off because

we're both in the Liberation Front, but he told me I had to do it by tomorrow or I'd get crucifixed. He was probably just being extra strict to keep the group secret, but it still didn't seem like much of a way to treat your 'rightful leader'.

I had to spend all evening doing maths again, so I didn't have much time to think of a plan for overthrowing Viktor.

If it were just up to me, I'd invite my old werewolf friends up here on the next full moon to rip his head off. It would mean we'd be rid of him, but none of us would be guilty of vampicide and have to report ourselves to the Vampire Council. And the werewolves would be happy with dog food and tennis balls as payment.

But there's no point in even suggesting this. I'm the only vampire in the world liberal enough to befriend werewolves. To the others, they're a bunch of flea-bitten fiends who are about as welcome on this island as the Pope.

The meeting is in half an hour, so I'm just going to have to wing it.

TUESDAY 18TH FEBRUARY

'Great news', said Lenora when everyone had arrived. 'Nigel's been working on a plan to overthrow Viktor.'

'Excellent', said Mr Dashwood. 'Let's hear it.'

I looked out at the black sea for a minute, in case any sudden inspiration struck me.

'I'm still working on it', I said. 'I'll definitely have it finished in time for the next meeting, though.'

'We don't need a plan', said Henry. 'Let's just tell the little squirt what we think of him and take the consequences.'

'No!' I said. 'He's more dangerous than you think. You have to promise not to tell anyone this, but when I was up in the throne room once, one of those blond vampires drew a stake on me.'

The others gasped.

'That's illegal!' shouted Seth.

'We can't let them get away with that', said Henry.

'It does indeed make things more serious', said Mr Dashwood. 'Why didn't you tell anyone?'

'I was afraid it would get back to them', I said.

'At least you've told us now', said Mr Dashwood. 'We must all work together as best we can to defeat the little tyrant. From now on, we must tell each other everything.'

I thought about owning up to my private blood supply, but decided against it. They'd only make me share it.

I noticed tears running down Lenora's face so I put my arm round her. It's a shame the others were there, as I'm pretty sure I could have converted it into a snogging opportunity if we'd been alone.

The Wimpy Vampire Strikes Back

Wednesday 19th February

Another weird blood feast in the throne room this evening. I got stuck behind Ron in the queue and had to listen to him going on about motorbikes. He always queues with his feet facing forward and his head facing back, so it seems rude to ignore him.

My sister and her stupid friends dressed up as cheerleaders and performed a silly dance routine. They even tried chanting the letters of Viktor's name, but spelled it 'V-I-C-K-T-O-R'. What sort of fan doesn't even know how to spell their idol's name?

They have absolutely no idea who they're messing with. Viktor could easily have thrown a tantrum about the inaccurate spelling and beheaded them. As it was, Svetlana grinned and applauded, so he smiled along.

The Wimpy Vampire Strikes Back

My sister spent the rest of the feast swanning around and fishing for compliments, but she got none from me. If she wants to suck up to the little demon, it's a matter for her conscience. I'm not going to encourage her.

Ezekiel and Abraham were just behind me in the queue and you should have heard them crawling to Viktor when it was their turn to file past.

'Allow me to thank you for bringing your remarkable leadership talents to our humble island', said Ezekiel.

'Your majesty', said Abraham, bowing before Viktor. 'I salute your courage, your strength and your nobility.'

Viktor waved them on and they swigged the blood. It was top-quality stuff once again. This one was a cold thick type B with a hint of vanilla, like blood ice cream. I can't wait for my sneaky flask of the stuff to turn up in the morning.

Thinking about it just then made my fangs extend and pierce through my tongue! I must have looked so dorky when I was untangling it. I'm glad Lenora didn't see that.

THURSDAY 20TH FEBRUARY

I've just thought of a plan. Svetlana kicked me off the throne because she found evidence that Viktor was the rightful leader. So why don't I try and unearth some evidence that he isn't?

Think about it: vampires are always squabbling over power. So what if Viktor is the rightful heir to our previous leader? That doesn't mean the previous leader took over fairly. It's pretty much guaranteed that he grabbed power by force or trickery.

Hopefully there'll be someone else in the coven with a rival claim, and I can back them as leader rather than having to take charge myself.

Whoever they are, they can't do any worse than Viktor. Unless my sister and her friends turn out to be the true leaders and make their vampire glee club compulsory, things can only get better.

11PM

I just went down the dusty corridor to the archive room. I turned the handle and found it was locked.

I'd never bothered to lock the door when I was in charge. No one seemed very interested in the place at all, as far as I remember.

I turned to leave and saw a figure a few feet away. I squinted into the darkness and saw it was one of the blond vampires.

'Sorry,' I said. 'I've lost my pencil case and thought it might have fallen down here.'

I ducked around the guard and darted away. I used my vampire speed to bomb up the six flights to my room, pushed my chair up against the door and jumped into my coffin.

Not that it made me any safer. If Viktor's guards wanted to stake me, this flimsy coffin wouldn't offer much protection. But it makes me feel better.

The Wimpy Vampire Strikes Back

FRIDAY 21ST FEBRUARY

We had another Liberation Front meeting tonight. They all loved my plan and were interested to hear about my trip to the archive room.

'It proves you were on to something,' said Henry.

'I agree,' said Mr Dashwood. 'He must have found evidence of a rival claim in the record book and wants to make sure we don't get hold of it.'

'So all we need to do is get into the room and grab the book,' said Seth.

'Great,' said Lenora. She leaned over to me and gave me a quick kiss on the cheek. 'Good work, Nige!'

A kiss on the cheek! Get in! I'm pretty much guaranteed a snog if I defeat Viktor.

SATURDAY 22ND FEBRUARY

I had crèche duty again today. There was a note taped to Nimrod's cot stating that the babies were to be fed no more than one bottle a day now. I can't believe selfish old Viktor has even put the babies on rations while he enjoys his fill of blood up in the throne room.

On the plus side, the rations seemed to have made the babies much quieter. This time they didn't try to jump out of their cots or crawl around the room. They just lay on their backs looking up at their skull mobiles and babbling.

There are no nappies to change with vampire babies, thankfully. Like the rest of us, they don't need to poo or wee. It would be a lot harder to get anyone to do crèche duty if that was part of the deal. Imagine having to remove a nappy full of steaming droppings. Ewwww! I don't want to be speciesist, but humans can be pretty disgusting.

At one point Nimrod's fangs came down and he started crying, so I picked him up and sang a traditional vampire lullaby:

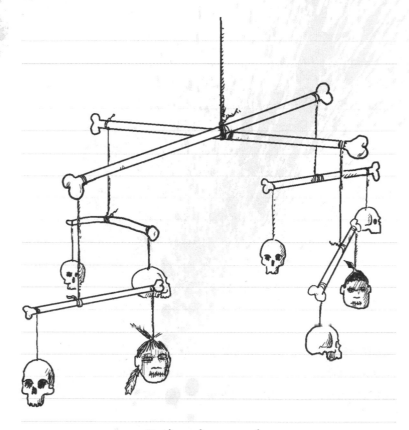

Rock-a-bye vampire

Hide from the sun

When the night falls

The human will run

When the hands grab

The human will fall

And down will come vampire

Sharp fangs and all

The Wimpy Vampire Strikes Back

I'll be the first to admit that my voice isn't exactly soothing, but it seemed to calm him. A couple of hours later, Zylphina started crying, so I had to fetch her doll. She'll need a new one soon. She's almost gnawed through the neck of her current one.

SUNDAY 23RD FEBRUARY

I need to find a way to get into the archive room. I think there's a set of keys in the drawer at the end of the discussion room – or throne room, as we must now call it. I never really bothered with them, as I was a progressive and trusting leader, but I'm sure one of those must open the archive room.

I just need to get into the throne room and distract Viktor for long enough to grab them.

Got it! I'll get my sister and her friends to perform a special concert in Viktor's honour. She can bring her CD player up to the throne room and dance along to her hits compilation. As soon as 'Don't Stop Believin'' builds to its rousing climax, I'll nab the keys and make for the archive room. Brilliant.

MONDAY 24TH FEBRUARY

My stupid sister has decided to put her own interests first yet again. I just went down to her room and asked her if she'd perform the concert for Viktor. At first she got really excited and started showing me all the moves she'd do. But when I told her to bring her CD player and turn it up really loud, she started getting suspicious.

'You're up to something', she said. 'You've got some sort of scheme to trick my poor darling Vik.'

Typical. My sister's meagre brain cells pick this moment to start working.

'No', I said. 'I just wanted to give you a chance to show Viktor how much you love him.'

My sister planted her hands on her hips. 'I don't believe you. And I'm going to tell the other Vikties.'

She made for the door but I dashed in front and blocked her way. 'Okay, forget the concert. It was a stupid idea. But don't tell anyone I suggested it. I can't explain any more, but it's for your own safety.'

'Okay', she said. 'But it will cost you a flask of blood.'

Fantastic. So now I've got to give up a whole day's blood supply. And as punishment for what? Oh, that's right, trying to help everyone in the coven, including her.

If all the other vampires were like her, I'd happily let Viktor run this place into the ground.

TUESDAY 25TH FEBRUARY

I've come up with a plan to get into the archive room that doesn't require help from any jumped-up little princesses.

I was thinking about the layout of the castle this morning, and I'm pretty sure the archive room is directly beneath the graveyard. It's four floors down, so you'd have to dig a long way, but I'm sure you'd reach it.

The Wimpy Vampire Strikes Back

All I need to do is get Henry to dig straight down from my grave. Everyone's used to seeing him working there, so it's unlikely anyone will take any notice of him.

We can take the soil away in our coffins, so a huge mound

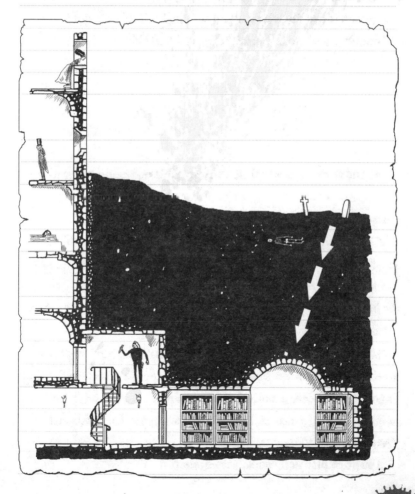

doesn't pile up. Some of the older vampires change their soil every day, so it shouldn't look too unusual.

I'm off to the Liberation Front meeting now to suggest it.

Wednesday 26th February

Everyone loved the plan. Henry was especially pleased that I'd found a way to use his grave-digging skills to over-throw Viktor.

We're going to empty our coffins into the sea every morning and take them to Henry for a refill. This means he'll be able to get rid of four coffins of soil a day, and should be done by the start of next week.

At the end of the meeting, Lenora came over and planted a kiss on my cheek. Let's hope there are plenty more where that came from.

This afternoon I emptied my coffin over the rocks behind the castle and took it down to the graveyard for Henry to fill. He's hollowed out a trench six feet down. The tunnel itself is going to be in the middle, and he's got a sheet of tarpaulin to cover it so no one can see.

I took my coffin back to my room, and I'm currently relaxing in the fresh soil. I can't believe what a vampire clichè I'm turning into. Next I'll become one of those vampire poseurs who talk with a Transylvanian accent even though the furthest east they've been is Great Yarmouth.

I vant to bite your neck. Mwah ha ha!

THURSDAY 27TH FEBRUARY

Dad came round and gave me a shirt and bow tie today. At first I couldn't work out what was going on, but then I remembered it was my transformation day. I've been a vampire for exactly 87 years today!

Happy transformation day to me.
Squashed humans and type B
Happy transformation day dear Nigel
Happy transformation day to me

It was good of Dad to remember, though it's a shame his gift options are limited to his own wardrobe now. The shirt

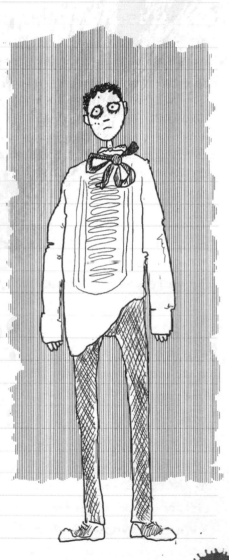

has a high collar and a row of pleats down the front. The tie is made of black silk and I think you're supposed to fix it in a bow, but I couldn't quite work out how to do it.

Neither the shirt or the tie go very well with my fashionable jeans and trainers, but I can't get away without wearing them at least a couple of times.

11PM

Lenora just called round and she said my new image was very 'gentlemanly'. I'm pretty sure that was a big compliment back in her day. Maybe Dad's gift will come in useful after all.

Friday 28th February

I changed the soil in my coffin again this morning. I'm sitting in it now and

Sorry, I had to abandon that last entry because my sister barged in and demanded the blood I owe her. I know I'd forgotten about it, but there were slightly more important things on my mind.

She was wearing a gown that was far too big for her, so it looked as though she'd been given a last-minute transformation day gift too.

I stood up and slammed my diary shut.

'What were you writing?' she asked. A smirk spread across

her face as an idea crawled its way through her mind. 'It was the name of a girl you love, wasn't it?'

'No!' I yelled. I tried to sound embarrassed so she wouldn't work out something much more serious was going on.

'Yes it was!' shouted my sister. 'You love her! You want to kiss her!'

I handed a flask to my sister and shoved her out the door.

She pranced away down the corridor, continuing her chant: 'You love her! You want to kiss her!'

The Wimpy Vampire Strikes Back

SATURDAY 1ST MARCH

I went round to my sister's room this morning to get my flask back. She was sitting with Amber and Ellie and painting a huge picture of Viktor with a hooded top and thick hair sweeping down over one side of his forehead. Nice to know they aren't letting reality get in the way of their fan worship.

They were all wearing 'I heart Viktor' T-shirts. My sister clearly hadn't left enough room on hers, because she'd had to write the letters 'o' and 'r' on the back.

'Nigel's in love with someone from this coven but he won't say who,' taunted my sister as I was fishing my flask out of the mess of glitter and glue on the table.

This sent Amber and Ellie into a fit of giggles. Ellie stood up, turned away and mimed hugging and kissing by crossing her hands over her body and moving them up and down.

If I'd known how unruly my sister and her friends had become when I was in power, I'd have been much stricter with them. They've been getting away with disrespecting their elders and betters for far too long.

When I'm leader again I'll make an example of them by placing them in stocks outside the castle and letting everyone lob holy water at them. At least that gives me something to look forward to.

SUNDAY 2ND MARCH

Henry knocked on my door early this morning to tell me he'd

broken through to the archive room. His face was covered in dirt and he had a worm wriggling in his sideburn, but he seemed happy enough.

He said he'd made a small hole in the ceiling at the far left corner of the room, which I should be able to wriggle through. I thanked him and told him I'd update him as soon as I'd been down there.

11AM

The sun's coming out now, which means the graveyard will be deserted. Time to head down and grab the evidence.

4PM

I returned from the archive room three hours ago now. I've been staring at this diary ever since, trying to work out how to describe the horror I saw.

I sneaked down to the graveyard straight after completing that last entry. The sun was rising over the crooked stones and everyone had gone indoors. I dashed over to my grave with my hands in my pockets and glanced up at the castle. No one seemed to be watching, so I leapt into the grave and swept the tarpaulin aside.

I threw myself down the narrow tunnel, bouncing off the wonky sides and shaking clumps of earth loose. I crashed down onto a bend at the bottom and a layer of fine soil sprinkled over me.

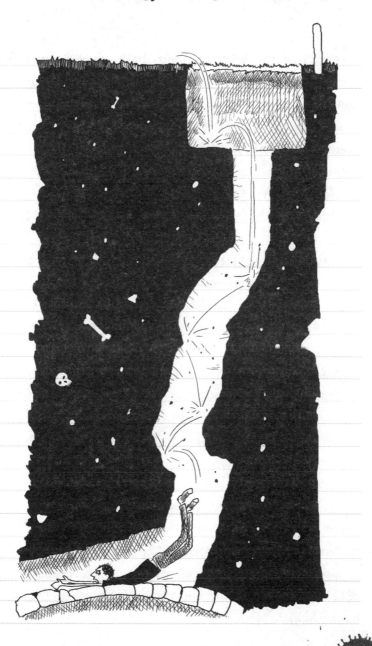

I scrabbled forward on my hands and knees until I saw a faint flicker coming from a small hole ahead. I squeezed through the gap and found myself on a high, narrow wooden platform. It took me a minute to blink the soil out of my eyes and realize I was on top of the bookshelf against the rear wall of the archive room.

I slipped down to the floor and got to my feet. The candelabras at the far end were burning, but the rest of the room was dark.

I tiptoed down the central aisle to the shelf where Svetlana had been looking at the record book. She'd left it on the floor near where she'd been standing, which was surprisingly careless. I grabbed it, tucked it under my arm and started to make my way back to the tunnel.

I heard shuffling from the front of the room. Was it possible that one of the blond vampires was in here with me? I hadn't heard anyone come in.

I peered into the gloom. The door was shut and I couldn't see any movement.

'Oooooooohh!'

I froze as I heard a loud wail echo around the vault. I remembered my sister's claim to have heard a ghost. She couldn't have been right, could she?

I turned back to the tunnel. I just needed to drink a pint of blood, have a nice lie down in my coffin and forget the whole thing.

The Wimpy Vampire Strikes Back

'Oooooooohh!'

The sound rang out again. I made myself walk towards it. So what if it was a ghost? I'm already Facebook friends with two werewolves, I didn't see why a silly spectre was anything to be frightened of.

What harm could a ghost do to me, anyway? You can't hold a wooden stake if your hands pass through everything, and it would probably hate holy water even more than me.

I forced my legs on towards the flickering candles at the front. I checked every murky shelf I passed for headless horsemen, angry wraiths and screaming banshees, but all I could see were piles of folders and books.

I approached the final shelf and peeked round it.

I instantly wished I hadn't. Why did I have to look? Why couldn't I have just taken the record book back up to the others?

Four men and four women were lying on hospital beds. Their legs and arms were tied with thick straps and their necks had plastic tubes sticking out of them. Blood was running down the tubes into wooden barrels on the floor.

The man on the left of the aisle, who had brown hair in a pony tail and bloodshot eyes, looked at me and wailed, 'Oooooooooh!'

I tried to shush him, but I think my fangs must have been down, because his low wail turned into a scream of terror.

This woke up a woman with red hair on the other side of the

aisle. She stared at me with wide eyes and opened her mouth to scream, but all she could manage was a raspy exhale.

Empty bottles of mineral water and protein shakes littered the floor. At the front of the vault, beneath one of the flickering candelabras, was a bizarre array of condiments and flavourings. There was salt, pepper, sugar, honey, some green leaves, some lemons and a spice rack.

My stomach felt like it was flipping round inside my body. I had to gulp to stop myself from spewing blood all over the humans. Then they'd really have had something to moan about.

11PM

No wonder Viktor has been serving such fresh blood. He's been keeping human cattle down there all along.

I should have known. I've never tasted blood like that before.

It can only have been produced by humans who are being force fed the same flavour over and over again.

Well, that's it. I'm not touching another drop of Viktor's hideous supply. From now on, I drink free-range blood only.

Time for a Liberation Front meeting now. I just hope I can put into words the obscenity I saw today.

The Wimpy Vampire Strikes Back

MONDAY 3RD MARCH

'I know why Viktor keeps the archive room locked,' I said when everyone had arrived on the beach. 'He's keeping human cattle!'

I waited for the others to gasp, but they just kept staring at me. I wondered if they were too shocked to react.

'There are eight living humans trapped down there,' I said. 'He's tied tubes to their necks to collect their blood. The very blood we've all been drinking!'

Again, I waited. Again, no one said anything.

'Don't you think that's terrible?' I asked.

'Yeah,' said Henry. 'It's a shame. But at least it means we get nice fresh blood. That's one thing the little twerp gets right.'

The others nodded.

'Right?' I asked. 'What's right about keeping those poor humans alive just for their blood? What kind of a life is that?'

'At least they get fed,' said Henry. 'And they've got a bed. I didn't always have one when I was a human.'

How bad must Henry's life have been for him to regard torture and imprisonment as luxury?

I turned to Mr Dashwood. 'Surely you don't agree with all this?'

'I admit there are ethical issues,' said Mr Dashwood. 'But it's hardly the matter in hand. What did the record book say?'

I hadn't even bothered looking at it yet. I'd brought it, but I'd assumed everyone would be too horrified to be interested in it. I handed it to Mr Dashwood and he started flipping through.

The Wimpy Vampire Strikes Back

I looked at Seth, hoping he'd back me up, but he just shrugged. 'I know it's bad, but I don't really care. I'm not that much of a human lover.'

Finally, I turned to Lenora. Surely she'd take my side?

'I'm sorry it's upset you, Nige', said Lenora. 'Maybe you can bring back the old blood-collecting method when you're in charge again. But worrying about it now isn't going to help us.'

So even my beloved Lenora didn't care about those poor

humans. Maybe everyone else had their conscience removed when they transformed. Maybe I'm some sort of freak for considering the feelings of humans.

Mr Dashwood shut the book. 'I'm afraid it's bad news. Viktor's name is mentioned in here as the rightful heir to the leadership of this coven. No rival claims are mentioned.'

Henry sighed. 'Looks like we're back to square one.'

TUESDAY 4TH MARCH

I tried to mope on my grave this morning, but all I could think about were those poor humans beneath me so I came back to my room.

My regular flask of blood was waiting outside my door. I felt like opening it up and tipping it out of the window. But then I worried that I might smell it and get thirsty.

Instead, I've shoved it in the back of my pants drawer. I shall now start a fast as a mark of respect for humans all around the world.

11PM

I've decided to put off my fast. It's probably best that I keep my strength after the shock I've had. But I'll make a start on it tomorrow.

It was that lemon blood today. There was a citrusy whiff around that woman with red hair. I wonder if it came from her?

The Wimpy Vampire Strikes Back

I don't want to think about it. I drank the blood for
sustenance, not for pleasure. If I made a loud 'Mmmmm' noise as
I was pouring it and muttered, 'That's the stuff' after I finished,
I was acting purely on instinct and cannot be blamed.

Wednesday 5th March

I was still worrying about the human cattle this morning, so I
went up to see Mum and Dad. I found them sitting around their
table, drinking blood and playing cards with Cecil.

The Wimpy Vampire Strikes Back

'I've got something to tell you', I said. 'But you must promise to keep it to yourselves'.

Mum put her cards down on the table and looked up at me. 'You're not bringing any more of those werewolves round, are you? I know it's good for you to have friends, but they make the rest of us very uncomfortable'.

'It's not that', I said. 'Viktor has imprisoned eight humans downstairs and he's using them for blood!'

Cecil slapped his hand to his forehead and pretended to faint. This made Dad laugh so much he dropped his cards.

'What other secrets are you going to share with us?' asked Cecil. 'That grass is green? That the sky is blue? That your dad can't beat me at cards?'

'You mean you knew?' I asked.

'Of course', said Dad. 'Viktor told us he was going to do it at the final Circle of Elders meeting. We told him it was a good idea'.

'Don't you care about the feelings of those poor humans?' I asked.

'Let me think', said Cecil. He poured himself a fresh glass and glugged it back. 'No'.

'It's very sweet that you care about human welfare', said Mum. 'But this is the real world, and sometimes hard decisions have to be made'.

That's right, Mum. Patronize me when I'm angry. Big help.

'I don't think it's sweet at all', said Cecil. 'I think it's ridiculous. You're not a carrot-munching social worker, Nigel. You're a vampire. Grow up and accept what you are'.

I looked to Dad, expecting him to step in.

'He's got a point', said Dad, taking another swig of blood. 'It's not as though humans care about our welfare. If they have even the slightest suspicion that we're near, they come for us with stakes and holy water. Is it any wonder we turn a blind eye to small things like this?'

I could tell I wasn't dealing with reasonable beings, so I ran out and slammed the door. I'm definitely going to start my fast now.

11PM

Just drank again. Cinnamon today. I'm not proud.

THURSDAY 6TH MARCH

Why am I the only one who cares about those poor humans?

Maybe it's because I've never been that badly treated by humans. One of them forced me to give him my lunch money once, and one of them refused to return my copy of *Sonic the Hedgehog* in 1991. But it's hardly up there with getting chased by torch-wielding villagers.

It might also be because I've had several human friends and even a human girlfriend. Most of this arrogant lot have probably only ever spoken to them as a prelude to popping their fangs in their necks. If they sat down and had a proper conversation with them, they might find we're not so different really.

Who knows? Maybe one day humans and vampires will live openly and peacefully together. They might even donate blood willingly if we put on a few vampire football matches for them. Who wouldn't want to exchange a pint for the pleasure of seeing Hirta FC scoring 3,000 goals against Manchester United?

11PM

Yep, drank it again. Honey flavour tonight. How can something so wrong taste so right?

FRIDAY 7TH MARCH

Mr Dashwood gave us a lesson on blood harvesting today. He took us through the three main methods:

1. Hypnosis and neck-draining

Pros: Traditional, no long-term harm to humans.
Cons: Blood can taste stale by the time it reaches a coven, high

risk of getting caught, especially since the invention of CCTV and camera phones.

2. Keeping human cattle

Pros: Steady supply of fresh blood, low risk of getting caught.
Cons: Minor ethical issues for those who believe in the fair treatment of humans.

3. Murder

Pros: Instant supply of fresh blood, victims unlikely to tell anyone.
Cons: Limited supply, major ethical issues.

I think he chose the subject matter as a way of apologizing for not supporting me more the other night. He went on for ages about how keeping humans as cattle isn't as bad as killing them, so I think he was also trying to bring me round to a more moderate point of view. He didn't win me over, but it was an interesting topic for a lesson, which was a nice change.

I'm not sure Mr Dashwood should have taught the lesson while rationing was still on, though. By the end of the lesson, nearly everyone's fangs had extended and you could hardly hear him over the rumbling of stomachs.

SATURDAY 8TH MARCH

Lenora called round this afternoon.

'Just checking how you're getting on', she said.

'If you could have seen them...' I said. 'The thin faces... The frightened eyes...'

'I know it was hard for you', she said, sitting on my coffin. 'But you've got to move on'.

I sat down and flopped my head on her shoulder.

'The only way you can save those humans is by overthrowing Viktor', she said. 'Then you can bring your old system back'.

'I suppose so', I said, wiping the corner of my eye. I admit I was hamming it up to get sympathy, but I am genuinely upset about the humans, so it's allowed.

'We're meeting again at midnight

on Sunday, said Lenora. 'Do you think you'll be able to make it?'

I looked up at her and nodded. She leaned forward and gave me a brief kiss on the lips.

She left and closed the door.

I got up, punched the air and poured myself a glass of blood in celebration. I now realize that this was an inappropriate thing to do. I was overwhelmed with emotion and didn't stop to remind myself where the blood came from. It's not a mistake I want to make again.

Still, a kiss on the lips, eh? It all goes to show that sensitivity pays.

SUNDAY 9TH MARCH

I've decided to focus my efforts on the Liberation Front again. But the least I can do for those poor humans is pay them one more visit and let them know someone's fighting for them. I'm sure that a few reassuring, friendly words will be a great comfort in their suffering.

7PM

That didn't go brilliantly.

I had to hang around for ages this afternoon, waiting for Hans and Eddie to leave the graves next to mine. It was reasonably sunny, so they shouldn't have been out at all. I think they just wanted to be sure they had good places in case it started raining. They gave up after about an hour and packed away their towels.

The coast was clear, so I dragged the tarpaulin back and jumped down the tunnel.

When I got into the vault, I slid down to the floor and listened for footsteps. It was just me and the human cows in there. I reckon the blond vampires only go down there in the mornings to collect the full barrels.

The Wimpy Vampire Strikes Back

The cows were all asleep this time. I wondered if I should rouse them for my reassuring speech, but I decided to give it a few minutes to see if they woke naturally.

As I was waiting, a strong smell wafted up to me. I looked across at a woman with brown hair on the far end of the row. There were crushed green leaves around her mouth.

I wandered over to her barrel and sniffed. It was mint! They were making mint blood! Mmmmmmmm.

I felt my fangs extend behind my lip. I used to love mint when I was a human. Tasting it again was going to be fantastic.

But I could wait. I was here to support these poor humans, not to satisfy my monstrous urges.

On the other hand, I had to pass the time somehow.

I lifted the barrel to my mouth and took a sip. It was more delicious than I could ever have imagined. I found myself lifting up the bottom and glugging more and more. It spilled down my T-shirt, but I didn't care. I had to have more.

A loud scream rang out right in front of me and I slammed the barrel back. The woman with red hair was glaring at me and shrieking.

'Whoops', I said, wiping the blood from the sides of my mouth. ''Scuse the mess. Anyway, I just wanted to tell you...'

'Ooooooohh!'

Great. Now ponytail man was wailing away too. I turned to him and tried to smile, but I ended up burping blood through my fangs. His low moan turned into a loud yelp.

The Wimpy Vampire Strikes Back

The other humans woke up and joined in the chorus of screams. I thought they might attract the blond vampires, so I shouted, 'Everything's going to be okay!' and ran back to the tunnel.

I'm not proud of how I behaved today. I wanted to give them hope, but instead I drove them into a frenzy of terror. But I swear I'll make it up to them. Next time they see me I'll be setting them free.

MONDAY 10TH MARCH

I must have had too much of that minty blood yesterday, because I had a really bad headache in the evening. It was just wearing off as I made my way to the beach for the Liberation Front meeting.

'I know we've hit a snag', said Lenora. 'But there must be some other way of ousting Viktor.'

'Let's start a revolt against him', said Henry.

'Yeah', said Seth. 'We can't be the only ones who want to get rid of him.'

'I think we might be', said Mr Dashwood. 'If history teaches us anything, it's that vampires will go along with the status quo if they're getting enough blood. And unfortunately most of our coven now associate Viktor with that tasty fresh blood.'

'Which is exactly what he wants', I said. 'But they wouldn't be so forgiving if they knew he had a massive supply of blood in the archive room and he could lift rations right now if he chose.'

'Brilliant idea', said Lenora. 'The next feast is on Tuesday evening. Wait until there's a quiet moment, Nigel, then call everyone to attention and tell them.'

Mr Dashwood grabbed my hand and shook it. 'Excellent. I think that could really turn the tide.'

I was about to point out that I'd only been brainstorming rather than volunteering to confront the mental blond vampires myself. But Lenora gave me another quick kiss on the lips and declared the meeting over.

It was nice to have another brief kiss, but I was too stressed to enjoy it this time. How did I end up putting myself forward for that?

TUESDAY 11TH MARCH

I can't confront Viktor. If I say anything about the rationing, he'll tell everyone about my secret supply, and my credibility will be staked to pieces. They'll be much angrier with me than him. But I can't back down. Lenora will never snog me if I wuss out.

It's amazing to think that I'm going to a feast of gorgeous fresh blood tomorrow and I'm not even looking forward to it. If you'd told me that a few months ago, I wouldn't have believed you.

The Wimpy Vampire Strikes Back

Wednesday 12th March

Viktor served a couple of barrels of that mint blood at the feast tonight. I'm glad the woman with brown hair bled enough to replace the stuff I stole. Seeing me might have quickened her heart, I suppose.

When the barrels were empty, Svetlana stood up and banged the side of her glass with a silver knife.

'Greetings, ladies and gentlevampires,' she said. 'To mark this wondrous occasion, the king has agreed to give a musical performance.'

The blond vampires clapped as Viktor took a wooden recorder out of his inside pocket.

He parped out a few raspy squeaks. I think it was meant to be 'Three Blind Mice,' but it wasn't easy to tell. It could have been '99 Problems' by Jay-Z for all I knew.

It was weird, because vampires are usually excellent at music. We've got loads of time to practise and our superior speed gives us amazing technical skill. I'm terrific at the piano, for example. But Viktor's effort would have been booed at an infant school talent contest.

He finished and looked up at the audience. Svetlana got to her feet and clapped loudly. The blond vampires, my sister, Amber and Ellie joined in.

Lenora, Seth, Mr Dashwood and Henry all looked round at me. I know they were expecting me to launch into a speech, but I couldn't bring myself to talk. Every time I tried, I glanced down at the holsters of the blond vampires and the words stuck in my throat.

I can't die yet. I'm only in my early hundreds. I've got my whole life ahead of me.

I was still trying to make myself say something when Seth suddenly pointed at Viktor and shouted, 'You keep loads of blood for yourself! We all hate you!'

Everyone turned to look at Seth. I saw Lenora and Mr Dashwood wincing. It was great that Seth had tried to make a speech, but he hadn't done a very good job of expressing our views.

Viktor sank down to his throne and began to cry.

'My son is a just king!' shouted Svetlana. 'He didn't deserve that vicious outburst! Take the swine away!'

Two of the blond vampires ran up to Seth and twisted his arms behind his back. Seth turned to look at me with his eyes widening as they dragged him out.

If I'd kept my promise, that would have been me!

The Wimpy Vampire Strikes Back

THURSDAY 13TH MARCH

Lenora came round this morning. She said that Seth's under room arrest and his rations have been suspended.

'I'm sorry I didn't say anything', I said. 'I tried to, but no words would come out'.

Lenora shook her head. 'Well, at least Seth spoke up. And I'm glad everyone got a chance to see what a little hothead Viktor is'.

'There you go', I said. 'It all worked out all right.'

'No it didn't', she said. 'Poor Seth's going to starve.'

I pointed over to the window. 'He's only a couple of floors above. I'll take some blood up to him as soon as the coast is clear.'

'Thanks', said Lenora.

I leant forward so she could kiss me, but she just turned and walked away. Looks like my cowardice has undone all the progress I made with her.

I hope she doesn't fall in love with Seth now he's a hero. He's about twenty times her age, though, so I doubt she will.

Friday 14th March

I went for a wander in the graveyard this morning and noticed that Seth's pyramid had been destroyed. Viktor obviously wants to send a message to anyone else who might be thinking of standing up to him. Seth will be really upset when he finds out, because he spent ages building it, and even painted some pictures of Egyptian kings on the walls.

No one seemed to be out this afternoon, so I thought it would be a good time to nip up and see Seth. I packed three flasks of blood into my rucksack, along with a paperback of Garfield comic strips. I thought it would be nice for him to have something to read, and he finds books with too much text difficult.

I put my rucksack on, climbed out of the window and leapt up to Seth's windowsill. I crouched on it and tapped on Seth's window.

The Wimpy Vampire Strikes Back

I felt really vampirey doing that. It's the sort of thing a sexy vampire on the telly would do. Obviously, he'd be doing it to some hot human girl rather than one of his friends, but it was close enough.

Seth gasped when he saw me, so I put on a scary face and drew my hands into claws for a joke. But this nearly made me overbalance, so I had to stop.

Seth was really pleased to see me, and was very grateful for the flasks. He tried reading the Garfield book, but it gave him a headache. I hadn't really thought about it, but I suppose Garfield looks a lot like that cat-headed god from Ancient Egypt. He's more like a man with a cat's head than a normal cat, especially when he stands up and folds his arms.

SATURDAY 15TH MARCH

I can't believe how apathetic vampires are these days. An innocent member of our coven has been imprisoned in his room. Where are the demonstrations? Where are the banners? Where are the charity fun runs?

I suppose it would be different if Seth had any family left. But his mum was staked by an Assyrian vampire slayer and his dad's head was ripped off by a Roman werewolf, so he has to rely on his fellow coven members now.

I bet these blasé vampires will regret their inaction when it's their turn to be starved or imprisoned. But by then it will be too late. There will be no one left to fight for them.

The Wimpy Vampire Strikes Back

Something major needs to be done. I think I'll write an angry poem.

9PM

I've finished my poem now. It's quite a departure from my old romantic style. It addresses two issues I feel strongly about, which are Seth's imprisonment and the human cattle. It makes for controversial subject matter, but if it helps change the attitudes of just one vampire, my efforts won't have been in vain.

It if changes the attitudes of two or three, that would be a good, solid result. Four or five would be great, and six plus is probably unrealistic.

STOP AND THINK
By Nigel Mullet, aged 102

All you daughters of darkness
And princes of the night
Won't you stop and think
If what we're doing is right?

Poor Seth is locked up in his room
And sentenced to starvation
Who'll set this innocent vampire free?
And end his isolation?

What about those poor humans
Trapped down in the vault?
What about their suffering?
Isn't that our fault?

The Wimpy Vampire Strikes Back

> Are we not all vampires,
>   Smart and fast and strong?
>   Why are we so slow to see
>   That what we're doing is
> wrong?

Pretty good, eh? I think that deserves a celebratory glass of blood.

SUNDAY 16TH MARCH

Mr Dashwood gave us a lesson on political prisoners today. He kept saying how unjust it was for anyone to be locked up for their beliefs. The examples he used were mostly from the

Vampire-Werewolf war, but you could tell he was really talking about Seth.

It was quite a clever way to protest about Viktor's behaviour. He didn't say anything that could get him into trouble, but he made everyone think about the issue. I used to think Mr Dashwood was stuffy and boring, but I've come to admire him since we formed the Liberation Front. He might be old-fashioned and strict, but he's stuck to his principles at a time when everyone else is letting themselves be ruled by fear and thirst.

At the end of the lesson I stood up and clapped. Lenora joined in, but everyone else just stared at us. They probably think we're crawly old boffins for applauding a lesson, but I don't care. There are serious things going on around here and all those sheep in my class need to wake up.

MONDAY 17TH MARCH

I spotted my sister wandering around this morning with a new Viktor T-shirt on. This one featured a scrawled picture of him playing his recorder. I told her it was outrageous that she was still worshipping Viktor after what he'd done to Seth. She replied that Seth was just jealous of Viktor's musical skills.

This is what tyrants do. They brainwash the public until they're so confused they can't tell incompetent recorder tooting from Mozart. I've seen this kind of mass delusion happen with humans, but I thought vampires would be too sophisticated to fall for it. Once again, my sister shows me just how low our species can sink.

TUESDAY 18TH MARCH

Another Liberation Front meeting tonight. It was weird without Seth there, even though he doesn't usually say much.

Everyone was impressed with my story of how I went behind enemy lines to deliver blood to Seth and my poem went down really well.

'A very powerful piece', said Mr Dashwood.

'That will really open everyone's eyes when you read it at the next blood feast', said Lenora.

Eh? I don't remember volunteering to do that.

'No', said Henry. 'We need to go further than words this time.'

'So what do you suggest?' asked Mr Dashwood.

'I'll challenge Viktor to a duel', said Henry. 'I'll defeat him, and demand he leaves the coven. No doubt his mum and those blond blokes will go with him.'

'A duel?' asked Mr Dashwood. 'How do you know his guards won't stake you just for suggesting it?'

I thought he had a point, but I kept quiet in case they reverted to the original plan of making me read out my radical poem.

'That's all for show', said Henry. 'I've met hundreds of vampires like them. They're full of talk, but when it comes down to it, they'd never kill another vampire. They'll be banned from

The Wimpy Vampire Strikes Back

every coven in the world. You think they'd go through that just to protect their little leader?'

'All right,' said Mr Dashwood. 'If you're prepared to take the risk, it's up to you.'

'I am,' said Henry. 'It's about time someone stood up to that little twerp.'

The Wimpy Vampire Strikes Back

WEDNESDAY 19TH MARCH

Henry was practising kung fu on the beach this evening, so I took a glass of blood out to him.

'I can't take your daily ration from you,' he said.

I didn't want to tell him about my secret supply, so I put on a pained expression and pushed the glass into his hand.

'You have it,' I said. 'It's important for all of us that you keep your strength up.'

'Thanks,' he said, and glugged it down. He handed the glass back and went back to practising spinning kicks.

I thought it sounded reckless at first but now I reckon Henry's plan will work. There's no way Viktor can win, and he'll lose the respect of the coven if he bottles out. It's against vampire law to refuse a duel, and Viktor will make himself about as popular as a werewolf with a crucifix if he tries it tomorrow.

THURSDAY 20TH MARCH

They served cinnamon blood at the feast. Everyone was going crazy for it, but I was so worried about Henry's plan I couldn't really enjoy it.

I think I must have looked even paler than usual, because Mum came over to ask how I was. I said I was worried about getting my homework done on time, which seemed to get rid of her.

After the blood, we were subjected to another horrific recorder performance from Viktor. I think he was doing 'Twinkle Twinkle Little Star' this time.

When he'd finished, Svetlana and the guards clapped. My sister and her friends cheered and whistled. That's right. Encourage him to subject us to more torture, why don't you?

I had a sudden urge to find Henry and talk him out of challenging Viktor. Seeing those blond vampires lined up behind the throne made me wonder if his plan was really a good idea. I started to think they might actually be crazy enough to kill for their little leader.

I looked around the crowd, desperately trying to spot Henry. I saw Hans, Mr Dashwood, Lenora, Dad, my stupid sister, Cecil...

I saw him, but it was too late. He was striding up to the throne.

'I have an announcement to make,' said Henry. 'You've taken control of this coven even though none of us wanted you to. You've imprisoned my friend for speaking out. And you're still rationing our blood even though you've got more than enough.'

Viktor's eyes darted over at Svetlana.

Henry jabbed his finger in Viktor's chest. 'And that's why I'm challenging you to a duel under the ancient laws of the Vampire Council!'

Svetlana got to her feet. 'Seize him! Let's show him how we deal with traitors!'

The blond vampires descended on Henry. Two of them grabbed his right arm, two grabbed his left arm, and one grabbed each of his legs. They held him down, while the

remaining guard reached into his holster and pulled out his wooden stake.

A loud gasp rang out from the crowd. Some vampires cowered back, while others shielded their eyes as though just looking at the stake would hurt. Even I thought that was cowardly.

The blond vampire held his stake above Henry.

Viktor jumped to his feet. 'Stop wasting time! Kill him! Kill the traitor! I am your king and I will not tolerate it!'

'So?' asked Svetlana. 'Do you renounce the duel?'

'No,' said Henry.

I was amazed at how calm he was. If that had been me down there, I'd have renounced the duel, declared Viktor the greatest leader in history and offered to give him my PlayStation and all my games.

Svetlana pointed at Henry's chest. The blond guard ripped his shirt open and held the stake over his heart.

At the back of the crowd, I noticed my sister running into a corner and throwing up. She was clearly far too excited. I have no idea why they allow her to come to these things.

'Now do you take it back?' asked Svetlana.

'No', said Henry.

The room was silent except for my sister's retching.

'We'll let this one pass', said Svetlana. 'But rest assured, we will not tolerate traitorous behaviour again'.

The blond vampire lifted the stake away and a wide smile spread across Henry's face.

I let out a sigh of relief. I couldn't believe Henry's gamble had paid off. It looked like those blond vampires weren't crazy enough to use their stakes after all.

Viktor sprang up. His pale face had turned purple.

'Don't let him get away with it!' yelled Viktor. 'Teach him a lesson!'

'Let's talk about this later, dear', said Svetlana.

'No!' shouted Viktor. He smashed his recorder on the arm of the throne. The top half split away and fell down to the floor. 'I'm king! I decide who gets taught a lesson!'

'Calm down, darling,' said Svetlana.

Viktor rushed over to Henry and raised the remains of his splintered recorder over his chest. He slammed it down, forcing the recorder through Henry's ribcage and into his heart.

Henry's eyes widened and he opened his mouth. He grasped at the instrument, then his hands sank down and his body froze. His skin tightened over his face, turning dark grey. It was such a horrible thing to watch, I thought I might have to join my sister in the puking corner.

A sound like a deflating tyre filled the room. I turned and saw the entire coven was staring at Viktor with their fangs drawn. They were all hissing.

Friday 21st March

No sign of Viktor today. He hasn't been seen since he pushed his way through the hissing crowd last night. He's probably sobbing in his room.

It's too late now. He can't take back what he did.

I spotted a couple of Viktor's guards patrolling the corridors with their hands on their holsters. No doubt Svetlana sent them out to quell any uprisings.

No signs of any yet, though. Everyone seems confused and

shocked rather than angry. If a vampire kills another vampire, their coven leader is supposed to restrain them and alert the Vampire Council. No one seems to know what happens if the leader himself is guilty.

I emailed the Vampire Council last night, though I'm not expecting much. They haven't even replied to my last one yet.

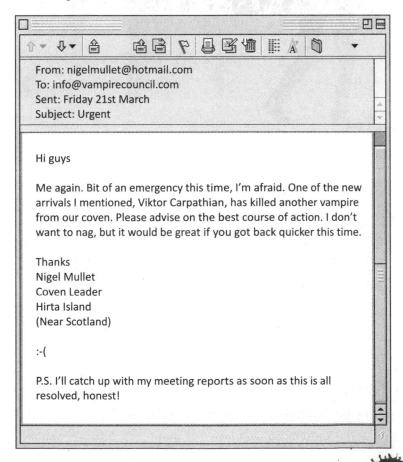

From: nigelmullet@hotmail.com
To: info@vampirecouncil.com
Sent: Friday 21st March
Subject: Urgent

Hi guys

Me again. Bit of an emergency this time, I'm afraid. One of the new arrivals I mentioned, Viktor Carpathian, has killed another vampire from our coven. Please advise on the best course of action. I don't want to nag, but it would be great if you got back quicker this time.

Thanks
Nigel Mullet
Coven Leader
Hirta Island
(Near Scotland)

:-(

P.S. I'll catch up with my meeting reports as soon as this is all resolved, honest!

The Wimpy Vampire Strikes Back

I helped Mike and Rob carry Henry's body down to his room this morning. We stuck it in his coffin and nailed the lid down. That's one advantage of resting in coffins rather than beds, I suppose.

Mr Dashwood is arranging the funeral for Tuesday, so the body can stay in his room until then.

My regular flask of blood was waiting for me when I got back. If Viktor thinks I'm going to accept his poisonous bribe this time, he can forget it.

10PM

It was coconut flavour today. That's a new one.

The Wimpy Vampire Strikes Back

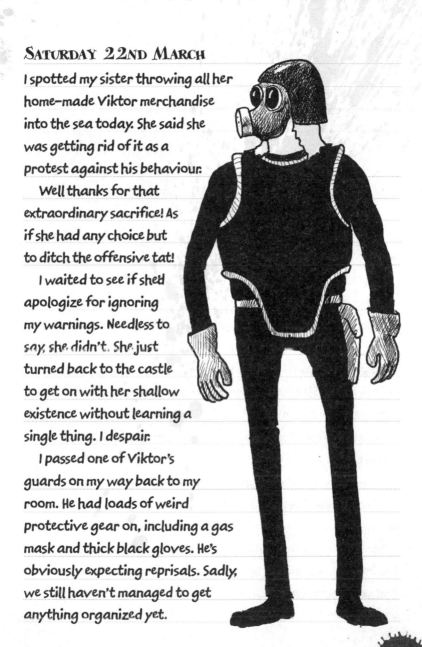

SATURDAY 22ND MARCH

I spotted my sister throwing all her home-made Viktor merchandise into the sea today. She said she was getting rid of it as a protest against his behaviour.

Well thanks for that extraordinary sacrifice! As if she had any choice but to ditch the offensive tat!

I waited to see if she'd apologize for ignoring my warnings. Needless to say, she didn't. She just turned back to the castle to get on with her shallow existence without learning a single thing. I despair.

I passed one of Viktor's guards on my way back to my room. He had loads of weird protective gear on, including a gas mask and thick black gloves. He's obviously expecting reprisals. Sadly, we still haven't managed to get anything organized yet.

HENRY HARTE
1792 – 1829
+
1829 – 2014

SUNDAY 23RD MARCH

I went to Mum and Dad's room today to ask what we should do. They were drinking blood as usual, though they were much less merry.

'It's a terrible business', said Mum. 'Covens are supposed to be a haven from that sort of violence. It makes me wonder if we should ever have joined one.'

'I told you he was trouble', said Cecil. 'Why did no one listen?'

'For the same reason as usual', I said. 'Because you didn't actually say it.'

Cecil just ladled himself another glass of blood. Even he wasn't up for a row today.

I snatched his glass away. 'Drinking won't help. What are we going to do about that little weasel on the throne?'

Cecil hissed at me and grabbed his glass back.

I decided I was wasting my time, so I went out to the graveyard.

Mr Dashwood was putting the finishing touches to Henry's gravestone. He'd done a wonderful job of cracking the stone and adding moss and lichen. I'm sure Henry would have been proud to raid it.

MONDAY 24TH MARCH

I leapt up to Seth's room today to give him some more blood. He seemed upset when I told him Henry was dead, but he didn't cry. I suppose you get used to vampires dying if you live to be 3,000. But I'm only 102, so I've never really gone through anything like it before.

I gave Seth a Tintin book, and he seemed to prefer it to the Garfield one. There's a talking dog in it called Snowy, but he uses all four legs, so Seth's unlikely to confuse him with the god Anubis and get a headache.

Instead of jumping back down to my room afterwards, I leapt five ledges across to Lenora's window. She was sobbing quietly on her coffin, but she smiled when she noticed me.

'Sorry,' she said, opening the window. 'It's all been a bit much for me.'

'Me too,' I said.

We sat down on her coffin, which she covers with a really chintzy white tablecloth. I put my arm round her and she rested her head on my shoulder.

'We shouldn't have let Henry challenge that monster to a duel,' she sniffed. 'We should have stuck to your plan of reading out the poem.'

'I agree,' I said, which was a massive lie. I'd have been the one with the wind instrument in my heart if I'd tried that.

The Wimpy Vampire Strikes Back

TUESDAY 25TH MARCH

We had Henry's funeral today. Black clouds swept in from the sea as we wandered to the graveyard. We couldn't have wished for a better day.

Everyone in the coven turned up except for Seth, obviously, Viktor, Svetlana and the guards. Ezekiel and Abraham dug a grave at the edge of the cemetery while Mike and Rob carried his coffin out and lowered it down.

We threw his possessions on top of the coffin in the old vampire tradition. He didn't have much. Just his shovel, a couple of spare suits and a skull and femur from his grave-robbing days.

Ezekiel and Abraham filled the grave in again. It must be awkward if a vampire with loads of things dies. My sister has so much useless stuff we wouldn't need to put any soil on top of the coffin. We'd have to stamp her glittery rubbish down just to get it all in.

Mr Dashwood stood at the end of the grave and gave a speech about Henry's life. It was mostly about his blood collecting and grave robbing. He didn't even mention

anything about Viktor killing him. It was probably just as well. Today was about celebrating Henry's life, not about rousing the rabble.

After he'd finished, I read a poem I'd written especially for the occasion:

IN MEMORIAM HENRY
By Nigel Mullet, aged 102

You used to steal bodies from graves
   Now your life has been stolen
      And you're in the grave yourself
         I think you'd have appreciated the irony
            If you knew what irony was
               But you were a very practical person
                  And weren't interested in that sort of thing
                     Nonetheless, we'll miss you.

I could tell that everyone found my poem very moving and thought-provoking. A few vampires were so upset they were openly cringing.

My sister must have been jealous, because she barged in front of me and tried to recite another funeral poem.

'Ashes to ashes, dust to dust,' she said. She paused for a minute, then continued: 'Sorry you're dead, have a nice rest.'

She was lucky she couldn't remember the real words because

they come from a prayer with loads of religious stuff in. She'd have given us all a crushing headache if she'd got them right, and for what? So she could be the centre of attention on a solemn occasion that had nothing to do with her. She wasn't even friends with Henry.

For some reason, loads of vampires clapped and my mum wiped a tear from her eye. It was probably a delayed reaction to my poem.

WEDNESDAY 26TH MARCH

Crèche duty again tonight. The babies were much rowdier this time.

Zylphina was making an awful racket so I picked her up and rocked her. While I was doing this, Nimrod managed to jump into Nathaniel's cot. I watched him sneak up on Nathaniel with his tiny arms held up and his fangs drawn. Nathaniel turned around, jumped in the air and smacked his foot into Nimrod's chest. I had to put Zylphina back in her cot to split them up.

It made me wonder about the nature of my race. Here were two vampires too young to understand speech. No one can have told them about vampire kung fu or neckfeeding. And yet they were battling away like trained warriors.

Is this conflict part of our nature? Are we doomed to fight? It's quite a depressing thought. I must remember to brood about it next time I'm in the graveyard.

At least there wasn't a werewolf puppy in there with them. Then I'd have seen some carnage.

Thursday 27th March

I could hear chattering as I made my way over the hill to the Liberation Front meeting last night. When I got down to the beach, I saw a huge crowd had gathered. I'm pretty sure everyone was there, even my sister. She always has to copy the things I like.

'Thank you all for coming', said Lenora. 'And welcome to the Hirta Liberation Front.'

'Can't hear you', shouted Cecil. Maybe the old duffer could have got a better position if he hadn't waited until the last minute to jump on the bandwagon.

The Wimpy Vampire Strikes Back

'Sorry,' said Lenora. She cupped her hands to her mouth. 'As you know, the aim of this organization is to kick Viktor off the throne, and restore our rightful leader, Nigel Mullet!'

Mum and Mr Dashwood clapped. It wasn't exactly the response I was hoping for.

'Who wants to get rid of Viktor?' I asked.

There was a bigger cheer this time.

'Of course we do,' shouted Cecil. 'But how do you propose we do it?'

Trust him to spoil my big moment.

'We're looking at options,' I said. 'I've already informed the Vampire Council, for example.'

'Those pen pushers won't do anything,' shouted Rob. 'You think they're gonna send someone all the way from Alaska to rescue us?'

'Let's go round to Viktor's room right now,' said Mike. 'There are sixty of us and nine of them. We can have them.'

'But they've got stakes!' shouted Hans.

'Then we'll make some of our own!' shouted Rob. 'We could have a hundred stakes each if we smashed our coffins up!'

A couple of vampires at the back applauded this.

'We can't fight a monster by becoming monsters ourselves!' shouted Mr Dashwood.

'But we're already monsters, technically speaking', said Hans.

This is why you shouldn't let everyone have their say. You get unhelpful contributions like that.

'So what do you want to do?' asked Rob.

'Let's just tell him we want him to go', said Mr Dashwood. 'He doesn't even know that yet. There's no point in resorting to violence before we've even had a rational discussion'.

'Let's have a show of hands for rational discussion', said Lenora.

Most vampires put their hands up, though I noticed that Rob and Mike made a big deal of folding their arms and tutting.

'All right', said Lenora. 'Discussion it is, then'.

'I agree', I said. As resistance leader, I thought it was important to say something, even though most of the vampires had already started their own conversations by that point.

Friday 28th March

When I opened my door to get my blood flask this morning, another of those small scrolls had been placed outside. I broke the red wax seal and opened it.

*As an apology for recent confusion,
you are cordially invited to a blood feast
in the throne room at midsnight.*

His Majesty Viktor Carpathian
and the
King Mother Svetlana Carpathian
shall be in attendance.

Bring your own glass. Formal attire.

Looks like we'll all get the chance to tell Viktor how we feel about him tonight.

I'm not looking forward to it. As soon as anyone mentions they want me back in charge, I'll be an obvious target. Maybe I should say I'm ill and stay in my room. Or I could steal one of the fishing boats and get out of here. I could change my name, get a job in a hospital and survive on blood bags. As long as I don't have to work with any nurses with especially attractive necks, I should be fine.

6PM

Rob and Mike just came round to ask what they should do about the blood feast. Why were they asking me? I'm not in charge again yet.

'Let's just have a discussion with Viktor,' I said. 'He might accept our point of view and leave.'

'We reckon we should go tooled up,' said Mike. 'In case things turn nasty.'

They pulled their jackets open to reveal crude home-made stakes tucked into their inside pockets.

I found myself jumping back from the horrible weapons.

'No,' I said. 'I shouldn't need to remind you those things are illegal. We're vampires, not smelly werewolves. So let's start acting like ones.'

I don't really think that werewolves are smelly; I was just pandering to their prejudices to get them on side.

167

'All right', said Rob. 'But don't come crying to me if his little lordship goes postal and we've got no way of defending ourselves.'

I won't be able to go crying to anyone, because I'll be the first one to get staked.

7PM

Seth just called round! Apparently Svetlana said he'd served his punishment and set him free this afternoon. Maybe Viktor's mellowing. It's far too late, of course. He can mellow all he likes but he needs to get off the throne and go and report himself to the Vampire Council.

The Wimpy Vampire Strikes Back

11PM

Time for the feast now. Here's hoping my heart remains unstaked...

??? of ???

I've just woken up. How is that even possible? Everyone knows vampires don't sleep.

It's dawn. I'm on the beach. I've got a massive headache. The beach is full of bodies. Waves are lapping against our legs.

Maybe Viktor staked us all last night. Maybe I'm a ghost now. I can't even remember if vampires can have ghosts. That's how confused I am.

Still ??? of ???

I've just seen Cecil and Mr Dashwood sit up and look around.

Now Hans and Ron are getting up too. So the rest of them aren't dead. They were just sleeping too. But how???

WEDNESDAY 2ND APRIL

I found out the date by looking on my phone. It took me a while to focus on it because of my thumping headache.

I'm not the only one who feels rough, judging by the groans and spews I can hear. How much did we have to drink? Is it possible to drink so much blood that you black out for days?

3PM

My headache is fading now, and by talking to some of the others I'm starting to remember what happened.

We went up to the throne room just before midnight, and the blond vampires ladled out some blood for us.

No one thanked Viktor this time, not even Cecil. I thought Viktor looked even unhealthier than usual, and the bags under his eyes had deepened. I hoped this was a sign that his conscience had been troubling him.

The blood smelled really weird, but I glugged it back anyway. So did everyone. Viktor was relying on our greed, and we didn't let him down.

It was disgusting compared to the other stuff. All around the room, vampires were wincing at the taste.

Svetlana stood up and struck the side of her glass with a knife.

The Wimpy Vampire Strikes Back

'My son is very sorry about what happened at the last feast,' she said. 'These last few days have been just as hard for him as they've been for you. He was in tears for a whole night after the incident, especially when I told him he wasn't getting a new recorder.'

Mike and Rob were standing at the front of the crowd and glaring at Svetlana. I was glad I'd told them not to bring their stakes, because they looked like they'd have used them.

'But the time has come for us to forgive and move on,' said Svetlana. 'What do you say?'

I looked over to Rob and Mike. I was expecting them to still be scowling, but they were clasping their temples and staggering from side to side. They looked like they were trying to walk down the aisle on a turbulent flight.

Rob screamed and dropped to the floor. Hans did the same, followed by Mike, followed by Mr Dashwood.

The Wimpy Vampire Strikes Back

'It's working!' shouted Viktor. He leapt from his throne and shouted, 'I'm not sorry I killed your horrid friend! I'm glad! I'd do it again in an instant!'

I was starting to wonder what was going on when it hit me. Bright white light flared into my field of vision and my legs flopped down to the floor. Stinging hurt spread through my body, freezing my limbs.

Next thing I remember, I was here.

4PM

I just left the others, walked along the beach and up the hill. As soon as I got to the top, I saw that a circle of high wooden boards had been erected, surrounding the castle and the graveyard. They were completely covered in religious symbols. There was the Christian cross, the Jewish Star of David, the Islamic star and crescent, and a squiggly bit of writing that I think is something to do with the Hindus.

The combined effect was like getting struck by a frying pan on both sides of the head at once. I threw myself down and waited for the thudding ache to go.

I didn't want to look at the barrier again, but I didn't want to turn back.

I closed my eyes and shuffled forward a couple of paces. I heard a twang and something sprayed up into my face. Holy water. My skin felt like it was on fire and I sank straight back down to the floor.

The Wimpy Vampire Strikes Back

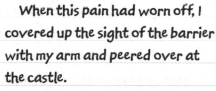

When this pain had worn off, I covered up the sight of the barrier with my arm and peered over at the castle.

A few feet beyond the barricade was a deep trench filled with wooden stakes. Some were long, some were short, some were sticking straight up and some had been planted diagonally. But all were very, very sharp.

I started to think turning back might be a pretty good option after all.

THURSDAY 3RD APRIL

Mr Dashwood has worked out what's going on. Viktor served us GARLIC BLOOD at that last feast! Ewwww!

One of those human cows must have been fed garlic cloves. It explains why the guard needed all that protective gear.

Vampires aren't supposed to go anywhere near garlic. The idea that we swallowed blood infected by it is just gross. No wonder we all blacked out. I'm more amazed we woke up after just a few days.

The Wimpy Vampire Strikes Back

The symbols barricade and the holy water traps are werewolf weapons. Mr Dashwood reckons Viktor must have nicked them from a pack he defeated in battle. They're incredibly dangerous things for vampires to handle. If the blond fiends had so much as glanced at the wrong side of that barrier when they'd been putting it up, they'd have done themselves a lot of damage.

It shows how serious Viktor is about wanting us to leave the island. We can't get past his traps and he isn't going to give us any more blood. We need to take the fishing boats to the mainland while we've still got the energy.

And then what?

We split up and try to live in human society again, I suppose. Aarrghhh! That means I'll have to go back to a normal human school!

9PM

Viktor's evil knows no bounds. I can't believe he drugged us so much we missed four days. Even worse, he did it over April Fool's Day, which I was really looking forward to. I was going to tell my sister that a vampire slayer was on his way to the island to kill her. I even mocked up a fake 'Wanted' poster with a picture of Van Helsing on it.

I bet she would have fallen for it.

Oh, well. I suppose I can try again next year in the unlikely event that we're both still alive and a visit from a vampire slayer is still something we want to avoid rather than a blessed relief from our miserable existences.

11PM

Mr Dashwood, Seth and Lenora just came over to ask me what human life is like now. They've all been in the coven for over a hundred years, and they're worried they might be out of touch with popular culture.

I told them about Starbucks, reality TV, Facebook, global warming, McDonald's, traffic jams and Gangnam Style.

They all agreed they'd rather be staked by Viktor than face that.

Friday 4th April

Nimrod jumped out of his cot today. He waddled down the beach and dived into the sea before anyone could grab him. I have no idea where he got all that energy. You'd think he'd be as tired as the rest of us.

We all had to flail around after him, which was a massive waste of our remaining strength. We all splashed and bobbed around uselessly, looking more like pensioners on a seaside trip than fearsome supernatural creatures. Eventually Mike grabbed his foot, dragged him back to shore and dumped him back in his cot.

Through the bars I could see Nimrod gurgling with laughter. I'm glad he enjoyed it. The rest of us were wiped out by his antics.

10PM

I just watched Cecil give Ezekiel and Abraham a survival lesson. He made up some ridiculous story about how he'd been shipwrecked on a desert island in the eighteenth century and survived by drinking fish blood. He went on about how he used to catch entire shoals at a time with his bare hands and squeeze them into his throat like ripe fruit.

Ezekiel and Abraham waded off into the sea to follow his

utterly worthless advice. They collapsed back on the beach twenty minutes later, having managed to catch a single fish between the two of them. Ezekiel stood up, held it over his mouth and crushed it. Gloopy liquid dribbled down. He swallowed it, grabbed his stomach and spewed it right back up again.

'You weren't doing it right', said Cecil. 'That wasn't the right sort of fish.'

Let's all thank our lucky stars we have Cecil to look after us. With survival tips like that, I'm sure we'll all be perfectly fine.

SATURDAY 5TH APRIL

We had a coven meeting this afternoon. We're all sick of hanging around on the soggy beach, and our energy is draining all the time, so we need to make a decision about whether to stay or go.

'That's our castle and we need to take it back', said Mike. 'So what if a few of us fall on stakes? If we all fall on the same ones, it might eventually create a bridge of corpses we can clamber over.'

I didn't think he was selling it very well.

'Viktor's giving us a chance to go and we should take it', said Dad. 'If we wait any longer we'll be too weak to travel back to

the mainland, and we certainly won't have the strength to hunt when we're there.'

I wanted to argue the case for staying and trying to find a way back into the castle, but I was too weak to speak. I'm sure I suffer more than the others when I haven't had enough blood. I think it's because of my sensitivity.

'Let's put it to the vote,' said Lenora. 'Who wants to try to find a way to confront Viktor?'

I put my hand up. So did Mike, Rob, Seth and Mr Dashwood.

'And who wants to go?' asked Lenora.

Everyone else put their hands up.

'That decides it then,' she said.

Hans ran down the beach towards the boats shouting, 'Women and vampires under a hundred first.'

Eddie grabbed his towel and followed him.

I really don't want to go back to the boring old human world. But I suppose we've got to go with the majority. If they sail off without us, we'll be trapped for ever.

SUNDAY 6TH APRIL

We haven't left yet. It turned out there wasn't enough space in the three fishing boats, so some of us are going to have to swim round to the other side of the island and steal Viktor's speedboat.

Nobody wants to do this in case it's protected by more holy water traps. So now they're all faffing around and trying to agree who goes in the fishing boats. I offered to rip up a page of my diary, write everyone's name on the strips and draw them out of a coffin. Cecil liked this idea, but Hans refused on the grounds that I'd pick my family members first.

No I wouldn't. I'd do the exact opposite in the case of one particular family member, in fact. A splash of holy water might knock some sense into her.

10PM

I got bored of listening to all the arguments tonight, so I wandered off down the beach.

I spotted Seth coming over the hill.

'Where have you been?' I asked.

'Looking around the barricade', he said. 'I thought there might be some gaps around the other side, but I couldn't see any.'

'Didn't you set off any traps?' I asked.

Seth shrugged. 'I suppose so.'

I stared at Seth. The lack of blood had obviously slowed my brain down, because it took me ages to remember that modern religious symbols and holy water don't affect him.

'Brilliant', I said. I grabbed his hand and pulled him towards the others. Cecil was arguing with Hans about 'rock paper scissors'.

'Everyone shut up!' I shouted. 'I've got a better plan.'

They all turned to me.

'If you're about to suggest alphabetical order, don't bother', said Abraham. 'I've already tried.'

The Wimpy Vampire Strikes Back

'It's not that,' I said. 'I've worked out a way we can get into the castle. The barricade and the holy water don't affect Seth. So if we curl ourselves into tight balls, Seth can carry us through the traps, and throw us over the wall and past the stakes.'

The Wimpy Vampire Strikes Back

'Then what?' asked Cecil.

I was so excited I hadn't really thought beyond this.

'We storm the castle and take the coven back,' I said.

I was expecting applause, but everyone just stared at me. I wondered if they were too weak to clap.

'It won't work,' said Cecil. 'Even if Seth can get us over the stakes, Viktor's guards will grab us.' He turned back to Hans. 'It's very simple. Everyone plays best of three against a randomly selected partner...'

Mike shoved past them and said, 'I'll come, mate.'

'Me too,' said Rob.

'And me,' said Lenora.

'You can count me in too,' said Mr Dashwood.

'Great,' I said. 'Anyone else?'

There was just the sound of crashing waves.

It looks like it's just the five of us taking on Viktor, Svetlana and the seven blond vampires. Five against nine isn't great, but it's got to be worth a try.

The Wimpy Vampire Strikes Back

MONDAY 7TH APRIL

I was glad Rob volunteered to go first. The lack of blood was really starting to get to me, and I was glad of the extra rest.

Rob crouched into a ball and Seth carried him up the hill. With his vampire strength it took no more effort than a human carrying a lapdog. I waited on the beach with the others, listening out for distant screaming and splatting.

Seth wandered back a couple of minutes later and said it had been fine. It was okay for him to be relaxed; he wasn't the one who'd get impaled like a cocktail sausage if it went wrong.

Mike went next, then it was my turn. As soon as we were up the hill, I could hear the traps twanging and holy water splatting on Seth's bare legs. I can't believe he can just wade through that stuff. I'd have been in tears.

I kept my eyes closed to make sure none of the holy water splashed into them, and I was quite surprised by how casually Seth lobbed me over the barricade. He didn't warn me to hold tight or wish me luck. He just chucked me over like he was returning a football to a playground.

I spun round and round in the air and landed on my head. I bet that would have hurt if I could feel pain.

I got to my feet. The last row of stakes was only about a foot away. Maybe Seth wasn't as good at throwing as he thought.

Rob and Mike were lying flat on the ground a bit further up

The Wimpy Vampire Strikes Back

the hill. At first I thought they'd been staked, but Rob whispered, 'Get down. The guards might see you.'

I ducked down and tried to get my breath back.

I heard traps going off on the other side of the barricade, then Mr Dashwood came flying over.

Seth had thrown him high, but he peaked too soon. He was hurtling down and it was difficult to tell if he'd clear the stakes or not.

Rob leapt up and ran over to the edge of the trench. He reached forward and caught Mr Dashwood just before he crashed down onto one of the sharp points.

Mr Dashwood opened his eyes, looked down and started to tremble. I can't believe I found him intimidating just a couple of months ago. He looked like nothing more than a frail and helpless old human now.

When the traps started going off again, I leapt up and stood next to the stakes. If anyone was going to save Lenora from them, it was me.

Seth threw better this time, and Lenora plummeted well clear of the stakes. I still caught her, though. She likes it when I do courteous things, because she's from the days before feminism.

I soon wished I hadn't done it, though. I was so tired I could barely keep up with the others as we made our way to the castle. It's not the ideal state if you're about to launch a ferocious attack on a bunch of supernatural psychopaths. Especially ones you couldn't beat even if you had your full strength.

It was weird to approach the castle again. It looked completely abandoned now, with its dark windows and closed door. Thinking about how Viktor was hogging the massive place for himself made me angry again, so I tried to use the rage to spur myself on.

As we approached the door, I heard something crack in the ground beneath Mr Dashwood. A plank with a wooden stake nailed to it swung up. He managed to swerve away in time, but his cape got speared.

Rob stepped over and untangled it. The stake was a couple of feet long, and tapered to a pin-sharp point.

'Vamp traps!' hissed Mr Dashwood. 'Even werewolves aren't barbarous enough to use these any more.'

The Wimpy Vampire Strikes Back

Mike prodded the end of it with his finger. 'Looks like they've been using a stake sharpener, too.'

The gate of the castle flung open and one of Viktor's guards dashed out.

'We need to split up!' hissed Rob. 'Let's regroup inside.'

I tried to sprint off, but I was so weak I could hardly go faster than a jog. Mr Dashwood overtook me, which wasn't a good sign.

The Wimpy Vampire Strikes Back

I glanced over my shoulder. The guard was hurtling towards me and fumbling with his holster.

I forced myself on. At any time, one of those vamp traps could spring up. But if I stayed still, the guard would catch me.

I tried to think of something good in case it was my last-ever thought. For some reason, all I came up with was an image of me in my old bedroom playing Connect Four against myself. Thanks, memory!

The guard was gaining on me. It didn't seem fair. He'd been enjoying a constant supply of blood, while I'd had nothing for days. How was I supposed to outpace him?

The comforting stones of the graveyard loomed ahead. At first my only plan was to duck behind one. It wasn't until I was actually among them that I remembered about the tunnel. This shows how the lack of blood was slowing down my brain. For the first time ever, my sister was only the second stupidest member of our family.

I scrabbled on, bumping into stones and slipping on moss. I grabbed the side of my gravestone and dragged myself round. The trench was still there, and the tarpaulin was in place.

I flung myself down and whipped the material aside. I let myself fall down to the bend at the bottom of the tunnel. An avalanche of mud followed me.

I landed on my shoulder with my legs dangling above as clumps of wet earth thudded down. I hope I never get buried

alive and have to spend the rest of eternity like that. It would be so annoying.

I knew I'd used up all my energy. If the guard came after me, I'd be unable to do anything but lie there like a useless old corpse.

2AM

As I tried to get my strength back, a thought moved slowly into my mind. Here's how it went:

'I wish I had some blood... They keep blood in the archive room... I'm next to the archive room... That means... That means... That means I could go into the archive room and drink some blood!'

Pretty thick, eh? You'd never guess I used to be in the top set for everything except science. But that's what blood deprivation does to the minds of even the most intellectually gifted vampires.

The thought of all that lovely fresh claret sent a jolt of energy through my body. I pulled myself along the tunnel with my fingers and squeezed through the hole into the archive room.

I flopped down to the floor and paused to check none of the guards were around. I heard nothing. It was just me, the humans and the delicious fresh juice of their veins.

I crawled down the central aisle, trailing earth behind me like a dying worm.

The human cows made a huge fuss once again. I suppose I

must have looked grim as I struggled towards the barrels. But I needed a drink and those crybabies were just going to have to deal with it.

I grabbed the nearest barrel and took a sniff to check for garlic. It was lemon flavour. Yum!

I rolled over onto my back and tipped the bottom of the barrel up. Blood splashed over my face and stung my eyes. It ran into my hair, my nostrils and down my cheeks.

The cows screamed even louder, straining at their straps and rocking their beds back and forth. I could hardly blame them. I must have looked like I'd stuck my face in a lawnmower.

I hoped the others were all safe.

Actually, that's not true. The shameful truth is that I was so distracted by my blood-glugging that I didn't give a thought to anyone except my big fat self. But the point is, I should have hoped the others were all safe. So let's just say I did.

3AM

As the blood filled my stomach, I found I could think straight again. It became obvious what I had to do. It felt like the sort of thing that should have been a big decision. I should have had a serious talk with Mum and Dad, read a Vampire Council guidebook and brooded about it in the graveyard for a few days. But I didn't have time to ponder. I just had to do it.

I got up and made my way over to the woman with red hair. She shrieked and cowered away.

The Wimpy Vampire Strikes Back

'I just want you to know that we'd be having a really big discussion right now if this wasn't such an emergency,' I said.

I grabbed the woman's jaw, lifted her hair back and sank my fangs into her neck. She fitted about in a wild frenzy, but I held her still and kept drinking. Her scream faded to a soft sigh and then to silence as her body fell still.

I unplugged my fangs and dug them into my wrist. Then I held my bleeding wrist up to the holes in her neck. I was worried I wouldn't know what to do, but it was all very straightforward. I just let my blood flow into the woman's veins until she started stirring again.

The woman opened her eyes and smiled at me. A pair of sharp fangs were newly visible, extending down from her upper gum.

One down, seven to go.

5AM

I did the women first. I thought I'd feel awkward drinking from the men, but I was so used to it by the time I got to them I didn't really think about it.

I collapsed back to the floor when I'd finished and poured a barrel of cinnamon blood down my throat. This time they didn't scream. They just smiled at me with their new fangs protruding down.

I'd always imagined I'd have kids one day, but I thought I'd be much more settled. I never imagined I'd have eight, and I

certainly didn't think they'd all be older than me. But we can't always plan the way our lives will go.

6AM

I untied the new vampires and gave them all a few sips of blood. I tried to avoid feeding them their own blood, though I had no idea if it would be harmful.

A woman with long black hair on the end of the row seemed to be the one who'd made the garlic blood, so I dragged her barrel aside. Accidentally feeding garlic to my kids wouldn't be the best start to my parenting life.

The Wimpy Vampire Strikes Back

'Listen carefully,' I said when they'd all fed. 'You've all just been transformed into vampires. That means you're all fearsome creatures of the night now. Okay?'

They just grinned at me. The one with the ponytail pricked his finger on one of his fangs and watched it heal.

I didn't expect them to understand me. It takes a while after transformation to develop into a mature vampire. But I thought I might as well address them in case some of it sank in.

I pointed at the door. 'Any minute now, someone's going to come through that door and I want you to help me attack them. Got that?'

There was no response.

10AM

The guard didn't come for another couple of hours. They obviously hadn't heard the racket when I transformed everyone.

'Attack!' I yelled, jumping to my feet and pointing at the guard.

They just stared at my finger and grinned.

'Go get him!'

The blond vampire undid his holster and pulled out his stake.

'I'll be very disappointed if you don't attack!' I said.

The blond vampire grabbed my neck and drew his stake back. Now they sprung into action, leaping from their beds and swarming on him. They stamped on his hands, pulled his hair

and slapped him. The one with the ponytail stuck his fingers up the guard's nose and giggled.

The guard opened his mouth and I grabbed the garlic blood and poured it in. He gurgled and spluttered, but enough of it went down his throat to knock him out.

I lifted him on to one of the beds and tied the straps.

As I was tying the last one, another of the blond vampires rushed in and we had to do it all over again.

12PM

Within a couple of hours, all the blond vampires were unconscious and tied to the beds. I had to wait for the guards to attack me every single time before my kids went for them. They don't exactly seem like fast learners, but I shouldn't judge them too soon.

I lifted up the garlic blood barrel and led the children

upstairs to the throne room. It took me ages to get them all there, because the one with the ponytail kept blowing out candles on the way. I told him to stop, but this just made him do it more.

Viktor and Svetlana were drinking blood on their thrones when I barged in. Svetlana was so shocked she spluttered blood down her gown.

'What are you doing here?' asked Viktor. 'And why have you brought that lot? I don't want human germs everywhere.'

'That won't be a problem', I said. 'Because they're not human.'

I pointed at Viktor, looked at the children and shouted, 'Attack!'

They just smiled and looked at me again.

I sighed and plodded over to Viktor. I grabbed his hand and started hitting myself over the head with it. 'Ow!' I shouted. 'Stop attacking me!'

It wasn't a very convincing performance, but it was enough to unleash the instinct of my kids. They lunged forward, dragged Viktor off the throne and stamped on him.

'Mummy!' shouted Viktor. 'Help!'

Svetlana turned and ran out the room. Even I was shocked at her shamelessness.

'Don't leave me, Mummy!' sobbed Viktor. I felt almost sorry for him, so I reminded myself of what he'd done to Henry.

Ponytail vampire shoved his fingers up Viktor's nose and I poured the garlic blood into his mouth.

The Wimpy Vampire Strikes Back

'I hate you!' he spluttered. 'You're the worst one! You're the ringleader! You made them all bully me!'

After a few more minutes of struggling and yelling, Viktor closed his eyes and fell still.

I heard Svetlana's voice echoing down the stairwell. 'Get off me! The king will punish you!'

Rob and Mike marched Svetlana into the room with her arms behind her back.

'Caught her trying to escape,' said Rob.

The Wimpy Vampire Strikes Back

'Excellent', I said. 'If you could hold her jaw open…'

Svetlana struggled and hissed as I tipped the last of the garlic blood down her throat. She fell limp a couple of minutes later and Rob and Mike threw her to the floor.

I heard a smash from the other end of the room and saw that the vampire with the ponytail had thrown a glass to the floor.

'That's enough!' I shouted. 'Stand in the middle of the room where I can see you!'

He smashed another one and laughed.

Lenora and Mr Dashwood ran in.

'What's going on?' asked Mr Dashwood. 'Are you sure it's safe to bring humans up here?'

'They're not humans', I said. 'I'm a dad!'

'That's wonderful news', said Lenora. She threw her arms around me and kissed me on the lips for at least a minute. Technically, I'm counting that as a snog. Result!

9PM

It took us a while to forge a safe way back to the beach. Rob and Mike had to dig up the grass and check for vamp traps. Then they had to drag the stakes out of the trench one by one, and kick a hole in the barricade.

While we were waiting I asked Lenora where they'd all been. She said they'd been caught and imprisoned in a room on the second floor. A couple of the guards had been stationed outside, but after a while they heard them leave. Eventually

The Wimpy Vampire Strikes Back

Mike broke the door down in time to see Svetlana fleeing down the stairwell.

Seth was still waiting on the other side of the barricade when we finally got through. He'd spent all night tramping the ground to set off the holy water traps, so it was safe for us to cross.

Amazingly, the argument on the beach was still going on. Hans and Cecil had settled on 'Rock Paper Scissors', but they couldn't agree on whether to play best of nine or ninety-nine.

'Viktor is defeated', I said. 'And I'm back in charge'.

There was a huge cheer from the crowd.

'Do we have to call you "king" now?' asked Hans.

'That's my boy', said Cecil, slapping me on the back. 'I knew you'd do it!'

'I take it we'll be celebrating with a blood feast?' asked Dad.

'I don't think so', I said. 'We should probably go easy on the remaining supply. Talking of which, I've got a bit of news...'

TUESDAY 8TH APRIL

Mum was overjoyed about becoming a grandmother. She beamed with pride as she watched the new vampires playing in the graveyard this morning.

She asked me what their names were, and I had to admit I didn't know. I suppose I could have asked them before I bit them, but it wouldn't have been much use, unless their names are 'Don't kill me!' and 'Why are you doing this to me?'

I'll find out as soon as they start speaking. After transformation, vampires go through a process of development before settling at their natural ages. So while babies stay babies, adult vampires go through mental states that resemble childhood and adolescence before reaching maturity.

Dad didn't exactly seem over the moon about being a grandfather. If anything, he looks on it less like gaining eight new family members and more like losing an unlimited supply of fresh blood.

The Wimpy Vampire Strikes Back

My sister got completely the wrong end of the stick about being an auntie, of course. She even asked me if she could hold one of them!

These new vampires will need our support to develop to their natural ages. The last thing they need is a ten-year-old girl cradling them and saying, 'Goo goo ga ga.'

The Wimpy Vampire Strikes Back

WEDNESDAY 9TH APRIL

This afternoon Mr Dashwood put on the protective suit and
lined nine coffins with garlic. Then he lifted Viktor, Svetlana
and the blond vampires into them and nailed the lids down. That
should keep them out of action if they come round.

He's loaded the coffins into the speedboat and tomorrow
he's going to take them to the Vampire Council's headquarters
in Alaska.

I think he's doing the right thing. Viktor has committed a
very serious crime, and deserves to spend the rest of eternity in
the Council dungeons. I suppose the others haven't quite
committed vampicide, but I hope they're severly punished too.
They all did their bit to overexcite Viktor and work him into a
murderous frenzy.

10PM

I've just had a thought. It will take Mr Dashwood ages to go to
Alaska and back, which means no school for months. Yippee!

It's just as well, because the kids are turning into a real
handful. That one with the ponytail jumped out of a castle
window today and broke his neck. You should have heard the
fuss he made while he was waiting for it to heal. It's the only
way he's going to learn, though.

THURSDAY 10TH APRIL

Mr Dashwood left for Alaska this afternoon, and Rob and

The Wimpy Vampire Strikes Back

Mike are about to take two of the fishing boats to the mainland to harvest some new blood. The last of the supplies from my vampires are running out, so they'll have to be quick. I need to find someone to take Henry's place on the blood collection squad, but I haven't had the time, what with the kids and everything. It's difficult juggling a career and a family.

FRIDAY 11TH APRIL

The kids have learnt to speak now. And I thought they were a hassle before! Every time I try to relax they swarm round and ask me stupid questions:

Why don't I need to sleep?

Why don't I feel pain?

Why don't I need to poo or wee any more?

What are my fangs for?

Are zombies real too?

Why is blood red?

I must have answered these questions a hundred times. They nod as if they've taken it in, then come back half an hour later and ask exactly the same things.

At least I've been able to find out a bit more about them. Their names are Josh (the one with the ponytail), Brad, Dunc, Chris, Kate, Pip, Jessica and Sara. The last thing they remember is stopping their speedboat to help a drowning boy who was wearing a suit and cape. They don't seem to remember their time in the archive room, and I'm certainly not going to bring it up. I won't hear the last of it when they reach their stroppy phase.

SATURDAY 12TH APRIL

Ron volunteered to join the blood collection squad today. I turned him down, which seemed to upset him. But what could I do? His back-to-front feet would attract attention, and every time he tried to chase humans he'd go the wrong way.

I offered to let him have the job if he chopped his legs off and put them on the right way again, but he accused me of discrimination and stormed out. At least, he tried to storm out. He actually bumped into my wall and fell over before leaving.

This is why I hate being leader. You have to make all these stupid decisions, and whatever you choose you're the bad guy.

The Wimpy Vampire Strikes Back

You wouldn't think I saved this coven from tyranny less than a week ago. They've already forgotten my heroism and started calling round to ask when the rations are going to be lifted.

I wish they'd ration their nagging.

11PM

I showed the children how to play *Need for Speed* tonight. They really enjoyed it, and Chris was so good he could almost beat me. I wonder if he played it when he was human and it's still in the back of his mind somewhere. After a while, Josh and Brad started fighting over the controllers, so I sent them all back to their rooms. It's a shame a couple of bad apples had to spoil it for everyone, and I hope they're feeling ashamed of themselves.

The Wimpy Vampire Strikes Back

SUNDAY 13TH APRIL

Lenora offered to help with the kids today. While Mr Dashwood's away, we're going to use his classroom to teach them the basics of vampire life. If we can get them to write the facts down, they might sink in and we won't have to keep repeating them.

Mum and Dad have offered to join the blood collection squad. I think it's a good idea, and will help to make up for their disgraceful behaviour under the Viktor regime. I'm going to suggest Dad wears jeans and a jumper, partly because it will help him blend in and partly because I know how much he hates it.

Ezekiel and Abraham came round to ask me when the rations were going to be lifted. I told them it wouldn't be long and they told me to 'get a move on'.

I can't believe how rude they are. Viktor mistreats them and the little slime balls do nothing but suck up to him. I treat them fairly and they snap at me like I was an incompetent waiter.

Maybe I should treat them mean and keep them keen. Perhaps when the blood supplies are topped up, I'll lift rations for everyone except them. Then they'd be thanking me for bringing my leadership talents to their humble little island in no time.

MONDAY 14TH APRIL

Rob and Mike returned with ten vats of blood today. They must

have worked really hard to get that much, and I made sure everyone thanked them as they collected their share.

The blood was nowhere near as nice as the stuff my kids used to produce, and I'm not just saying that out of parental pride. It's much staler, and it's just plain old blood, without any fancy flavouring. But we're all going to have to get used to it. We won't be using any more human cattle while I'm in charge.

11PM

The children have lost their milk fangs now. They came to show me the gaps in their mouths this evening. Brad even pulled his out in front of me, and I told him to leave them under his coffin for the tooth demon.

They'll have their permanent fangs by this time tomorrow. I can't believe how fast they're growing up!

The Wimpy Vampire Strikes Back

TUESDAY 15TH APRIL

We gave the children a lesson about blood today. I explained that they'd usually have to run around after humans and bite their necks to get it, but we provide it for free. I hope this helped them realize how easy they have it in a coven.

Lenora handed out a worksheet where they had to answer questions about different blood types. She went round to help whenever they stuck their hands up, and was really patient with their stupid questions.

After they'd gone I thanked her for helping me out, and she said I was a wonderful dad. Then we had a proper snog! I'd better not write much about it, though. She's very old-fashioned and I don't think she'd like it if I did.

I think we're sort of going out now. I haven't actually said anything, but it feels like we are. We spent ages chatting in her room last night, and she didn't seem uncomfortable about me being in her room so late.

WEDNESDAY 16TH APRIL

I must be officially going out with Lenora, because Brad called her 'Mum' in class today, and she didn't correct him.

We were giving them a safety lesson about garlic, holy water and stakes. Josh and Brad kept whispering things to each other and giggling, so I had to separate them.

I told them they wouldn't find it funny if a vampire slayer walloped a stake into their hearts, and this seemed to shut them up. Ultimately, all I can do is warn them. If they don't want to listen, it's up to them.

Seth has now finished burning the barrier and all the stakes, so he came round tonight to help me catch up on my paperwork. He isn't very fast at reading or writing, but he tries really hard. I told him what had happened in the last few Circle of Elders meetings and he attempted to fill in the report forms.

He wrote the first couple backwards, so I made him do them again. He wasn't trying to be weird, it's just that they used to write from right to left in his day.

The Wimpy Vampire Strikes Back

I'm not going to fill in any reports about the siege, as I'm sure Mr Dashwood will tell the council all about it. Plus, the questions are all things like, 'How did you resolve the issue?' and 'How do you think you handled your responsibility?' There are no questions like, 'Did a psychopathic child murder one of your friends with a musical instrument?'

Thursday 17th April

Mum and Dad brought some more blood back from the mainland today, so I was able to officially lift rations.

I expected a stream of grateful coven members to call round but the only vampire who came to congratulate me was Lenora.

I've barely even started on my list of stuff to do. I've got to rebuild Seth's pyramid, convert the throne room back into the

discussion room and get Mrs Dean to resume her cleaning round, and that's just for starters. But when Lenora invited me for a walk in the graveyard, I agreed to throw my list aside. It's not as if anyone's going to thank me anyway.

When we were outside, I asked Lenora if I was allowed to call her my girlfriend, and she agreed. Heavy rain started to fall and we had a kiss. It was a wonderful romantic moment, but unfortunately the weather drew Hans and Eddie out, which killed the mood.

Friday 18th April

I gave the kids a lesson about werewolves today. I had to make it very biased and say that all werewolves are evil. It's not true, and I felt slightly ashamed of myself, but you have to exaggerate when you're talking to new vampires. If they go around petting every one they see, they'll get their heads ripped off in no time.

The children behaved much better today. They all took notes, listened attentively and asked sensible questions about full moon safety. They seem much more grown up now, which is a shame because it means their stroppy phase will be along soon.

Saturday 19th April

Today I appointed Seth as deputy leader. He's agreed to take over most of the decision-making and paperwork, which should free me up to spend more time with Lenora and unlock some new cars on *Need for Speed*. He's effectively in charge now, but I'm still going to hold the official position of leader for the sake of stability.

I've appointed Cecil, Hans and Ron as the new Circle of Elders, and I've told them to help Seth with writing the reports. Ron was really pleased when I chose him. I hope it proved I'm not discriminating against him. I'm quite happy for him to have a job that doesn't involve walking in the right direction.

SUNDAY 20TH APRIL

Whoops! I was checking through my email spam folder today when I saw these:

The Wimpy Vampire Strikes Back

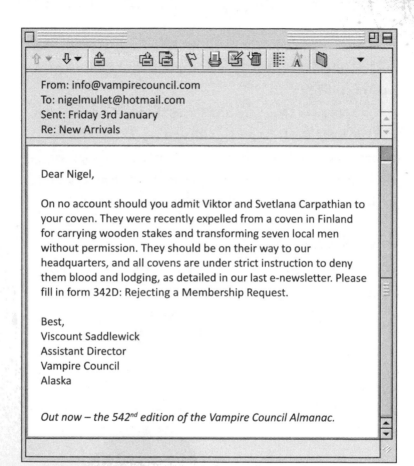

From: info@vampirecouncil.com
To: nigelmullet@hotmail.com
Sent: Friday 3rd January
Re: New Arrivals

Dear Nigel,

On no account should you admit Viktor and Svetlana Carpathian to
your coven. They were recently expelled from a coven in Finland
for carrying wooden stakes and transforming seven local men
without permission. They should be on their way to our
headquarters, and all covens are under strict instruction to deny
them blood and lodging, as detailed in our last e-newsletter. Please
fill in form 342D: Rejecting a Membership Request.

Best,
Viscount Saddlewick
Assistant Director
Vampire Council
Alaska

Out now – the 542nd edition of the Vampire Council Almanac.

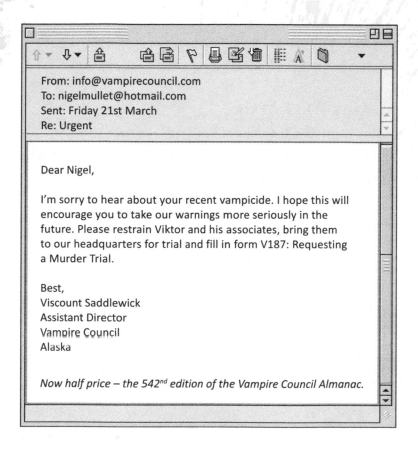

From: info@vampirecouncil.com
To: nigelmullet@hotmail.com
Sent: Friday 21st March
Re: Urgent

Dear Nigel,

I'm sorry to hear about your recent vampicide. I hope this will encourage you to take our warnings more seriously in the future. Please restrain Viktor and his associates, bring them to our headquarters for trial and fill in form V187: Requesting a Murder Trial.

Best,
Viscount Saddlewick
Assistant Director
Vampire Council
Alaska

Now half price – the 542nd edition of the Vampire Council Almanac.

I think I'll delete the emails and pretend I didn't get them. It's annoying that I could have saved myself all that hassle just by checking my spam folder. Having said that, I probably wouldn't be going out with Lenora if none of it had happened, so perhaps it was all for the best.

We had another lovely stroll in the graveyard this morning. Rob's rebuilt Seth's pyramid and filled in my grave again.

The Wimpy Vampire Strikes Back

He asked me if I wanted to replace the reservation stone, but I told him to leave it. I think I deserve some small privileges.

MONDAY 21ST APRIL

Just as I expected, the children have entered their stroppy phase now. I went to fetch them this morning, and none of them would budge from their coffins.

'Why don't you go to school if you like it so much?' yelled Brad, slamming his lid closed.

Kate rolled over in her soil and muttered, 'I don't have to do what you say. You're not even my real dad!'

Josh threw his exercise book at me and shouted, 'I didn't ask to be transformed!'

I cancelled their lessons. There's no point in trying to teach them when they're like this.

It's all very odd. When I first transformed them I couldn't

wait for them to grow up and become independent. Now I wish they could have stayed in their last phase a little longer. But I suppose I'm just going to have to put up with it.

I can't complain. I've been going through my stroppy teenage phase for nine decades now.

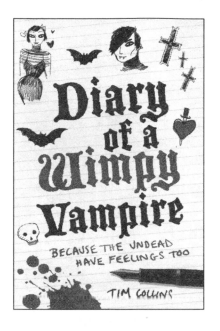

Diary of a Wimpy Vampire: Because the
undead have feelings too

978-1-84317-458-5 in paperback print format
978-1-84317-611-4 in ePub format
978-1-84317-612-1 in Mobipocket format

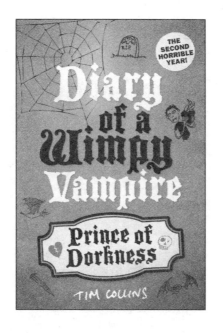

Diary of a Wimpy Vampire:
Prince of Dorkness

978-1-84317-524-7 in paperback print format
978-1-84317-648-0 in ePub format
978-1-84317-649-7 in Mobipocket format

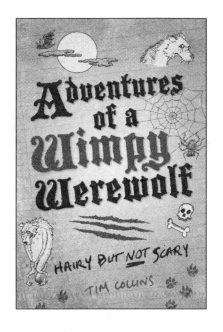

Adventures of a Wimpy Werewolf:
Hairy but not scary

978-1-84317-856-9 in paperback print format
978-1-84317-858-3 in ePub format
978-1-84317-857-6 in Mobipocket format

Find *Diary of a Wimpy Vampire* on Facebook,
and follow Nigel on Twitter (@NigelTheVampire).